'WHEN THE DAWN BREAKS'

'WHEN THE DAWN BREAKS'

The Collection

MARY ANN MCPHEDRAN

authorHOUSE®

AuthorHouse™ UK Ltd.
1663 Liberty Drive
Bloomington, IN 47403 USA
www.authorhouse.co.uk
Phone: 0800.197.4150

Published by AuthorHouse 07/29/2014

ISBN: 978-1-4969-8711-2 (sc)
ISBN: 978-1-4969-8712-9 (e)

I dedicate this book to;

To Jackie and Gareth for making my Reunion
with my best friend at their home in Cyprus
a great success, and a wonderful holiday.
To Mary for being there for me..

Joe and Kate were going steady and were planning to get engaged, but before settling down they decided they would like to go travelling around Greece.

"When are we going to do this travelling thing?" said Kate.

"No time like the present." Joe answered and after pausing he went on to say,

"I think we should put our notice in on Monday ready to leave by the time the factory breaks for the annual holiday."

She agreed with him and they both decided to give their notice to leave their jobs on Monday.

Kate was waiting at the gate. She was waiting for Mary coming up the hill.

"Are you sickening for something you're not usually early on a Monday?" she said when she saw Kate waiting.

"Oh I'm too excited I'm going to Greece with Joe."

"I thought you were saving, and getting engaged during the holiday period?"

"I am, but we have agreed to go travelling. I'm putting my notice in to leave."

"You're gallivanting around Greece? God my maw would have a fit if I came in and said that I was going to travel instead of working."

Kate was fed up by Mary's continuing questions and said no more. They spent the rest of the journey to work in silence. Kate noticed a little envy in Mary's reaction to her news.

Joe was waiting for Kate when she arrived home from work

"I hope you have put your notice in because I have?" Kate nodded that she had and he picked her up and swung her around the room. Her parents looked at them and her Mother shook her head. There was no point in arguing because she would go anyway.

The next two weeks were spent planning what to take with them. Kate wanted everything in her wardrobe and Joe had to remind her it was a back pack and she would be carrying it around with her. Travelling from place to own to Joe wondered how Kate would cope with the reality of back packing. She never had to go without and share rough conditions. She eventually agreed to what he was saying. The last week was buying the things they needed for their trip and to catch up with their friend before leaving to go on their trip. Eventually the day came and it was time to leave.

A quick exit saying goodbye to her Mother, she gave her a hug, and was heading out the door to meet Joe. Saturday morning they went to the train station in Peterborough and caught the eight forty five to Gatwick airport and they were on their first leg of the journey to Greece' When arriving in the Airport and going straight to the coffee bar.

"I'm starving."

"So am I" Joe answered and ordered breakfast.

After breakfast they picked up some products that had been forgotten from the news agent and Boots the Chemist. A few hours later on their way to zany,

Joe didn't like the flight as it was a little bumpy going through the clouds. It was only for a few minutes and he settled down.

"Do you want a drink?" Joe asked when the trolley selling all sorts appeared in front of us.

"Yes I will have vodka."

"A vodka and coke twice," he said to the hostess, and she gave him the drinks. He was watching TV and he soon forgot about his fear of flying. They were soon boarding the bus to take them to where they booked into ' Christina apartment.'

MAKING PLANS

The apartment wasn't much to look at, it was very basic. There were twin beds, two bedside cabinets and a dresser against the wall. The kitchen area had a stove and a small area next to the kitchen was the shower room.

Kate turned her nose up at it, and Joe remarked

"You will be living in worse conditions than this by the time this trip is over. Just accept it."

Kate saw something in Joe that she hadn't seen before. Did she detect that he was being a little bossy?

She looked at him and gave him a warning look. He must have read her mind, he gave her a hug. He walked over to the beds and pushed them together

"It's not going to be all sweetness and pretty sights, there are going to be some rough times ahead." defending his actions. He was about to draw her close to him when the owner of the apartment came to the door with some towels. She introduced herself as Christina. She looked at the beds pushed together, and said she would get them replaced with a double bed...

Joe's moment had passed; He decided they would go to the shop. Kate was a little embarrassed and her face flushes. She made an excuse to go to the bathroom.

She was apprehensive about sleeping with him; they had sex before but not as intimate. She had never spent the night with him.

He called to her." Come on let's go and buy you that ring before the shops close." She finished tidying her hair and went to join him.

Kate looked at several rings before making her choice.

She chose a single diamond. Joe decided he would not have a ring. He would have one when they get married. He paid the bill and they went on to restaurant. They had a splendid meal and a bottle of wine to mark the occasion, and had an enjoyable evening.

They returned to their apartment, and were surprised to see a bottle of wine and two glasses with a little card saying congratulation compliments from Christiana.

"She must have heard you saying about the ring, how sweet." She looked across and she saw the double bed, but never made any remark about it. Joe opened the wine and poured two glasses.

Joe gave her that longing look and suggested they have a shower together Kate reminded him to lock the door. He locked the door and took her by the hand to the shower room. They removed their clothes and Kate allowed Joe to wash her all over. He took her breasts in his hand, gently caressing, them and kissing her tender nipples. He felt himself being aroused, he lifted her on to the bed, and they made passionate love. When it was over they had a glass of wine, and raised their glasses and together they said "cheers."

***

Out And About

Next morning Kate opened her eyes to the sunshine streaming through the window. She looked to see if Joe was awake, but he was still sleeping. She moved gently out of the bed so not to disturb him. She went to the shower room and quickly washed and dressed. She looked at the shower and last night's memories of events came rushing back to her. She blushed and then thought about their seductive actions, and said to herself.

"It was nice a perfect ending to her celebrations of their engagement." she also reminded that she would have to be careful and make sure she takes the contraceptive pill. It was her Mother's last piece of advice before leaving home for the trip.

Her train of thought was disturbed when she heard Joe call for her.

"Oh your dressed I wanted to cuddle you," and with a longing look he coaxed her back to bed and they engaged in passionate love making. After he smoked a cigarette and they lay planning the day events. They decided that they would hire some bikes today and tomorrow they would explore the different places of interest in Zanty.

While Joe was getting dressed she went out to the balcony. Two girls were sitting reading on the next door balcony. She nodded to them and after a few moments she went out of the apartment to the beach

The beach was only a short distance from the apartment. Kate was eager to get into the water and rushed the last few meters to enter on to it. They stood shocked at the sight in front of them. A double Decker bus was in service along the sand. It was picking up passengers and dropping them off. They picked a spot on the sand and ordered two sunbeds and umbrella. The bathers were in the water and the tide was low. The water only came up to their waists.

She stripped down to her swim wear, which she was wearing under her shorts and T shirt, and went into the sea. Joe called and made a joke. "Don't forget to look left and right or is it right and left here in Zany." when she was going into the water.

Joe and Kate spent about four hours on the beach. The two girls who were living next door to them were passing by. They stopped to say hello and talk. The girls suggested that Kate and Joe come along to the bar where they work. It was Antonio's bar, where they handed out flyers and to entice the customers to go in. Seemed very friendly and Joe said he would look in

"By the way our names are Rose and Jean." And they pointed to who was who. They changed from their swimming outfits into shorts and tee shirts.

And went for some food to take back to the apartment. They chose a ready cooked chicken salad, with crusty bread for their dinner.

After dinner Kate went to have her shower and Joe offered to join her but Kate stopped him in his tracks.

"No if I'm going out tonight I need quality time, to myself, to get ready."

"Are you sure he said holding her close to him." But

She made no move to encourage him and went to the shower. On her own. While Kate was in the shower he made a vodka and coke for both of them

She looked at her clothes from the wardrobe and chose a cream pair of crop trousers and a lemon Shirt with cream sandals.

After she was finished showering Joe went into shower and get dressed to go out to the bar.

It was heaving with customers outside and Joe made his way inside to find a table and ordered some drinks. A drag queen came on to entertain and he was Tina Turner, and he sang all her top hits.

Kate remarked that he was just like Tina singing, and Joe said he was miming to a tape. He was very good and the night out was a success. They walked back home in the pleasant warm air.

Joe wakened early in the morning; he turned to look to see if Kate was awake, and he snuggled close to her. She didn't respond, so he gently eased himself out of the bed, taking care not to disturb her. He quickly washed and dressed; then slipped out of the apartment.

He was walking along the sand when a huge dog came bounding towards him. At first he was alarmed at the size of the do, and when the dog licked his hand, he returned the friendly gesture by patting him on the head.

"Where did you come from?" and he continued to rub his head before going on with his walk. He hadn't gone far when a car screeched to a halt before him.

Bloody time shares, why can't they leave people alone to enjoy their holiday?" He muttered to himself thinking they were Time Shares agents.

He turned away from them, and they persisted in following until the car was level with him. His instinct told him that he was in danger. The man sitting in the passenger seat started to come out of the car. Joe was about to run but the dog leaped at the man, and he jumped back into the car screaming.

"Drive." he said. For pity sake let's get out of here."

I am. I can't turn the car. The wheels are not turning in the sand."

At that moment the dog was snarling and showing his teeth.

The car went into gear and sped off down towards the town.

Joe was a little shaken by the events, and decided to go home in case they come back. The dog turned and went in the other direction. He turned, as if to look, to see if Joe was following him.

Joe was trying to make sense of the episode and he shuddered to think what might have happened if the dog had not went with him walking.

"Yes someone up there was looking after me. He thought.

"Did God send me a Guardian Angel?" He muttered and made his way home he went into a shop where you can hire bikes, and put the deposit down to hire the bikes for a week...

OUT AND ABOUT
ON A BIKE

Kate was out of bed and washed dressed and waiting for Joe.

"Where have you been I have been? waiting for ages for you."

"I went for a walk and was nearly attacked by two men."

He told Kate about the dog and the car. Kate thought that it was the rucksack that they were drawing attention to the fact that they were traveling around Greece and carrying enough money to support the trip.

"I have booked the bikes and we can go and choose them when you are ready."

When they picked up the bikes they had been given a map and a protective helmet. The bikes had two bags attached to them, and a saddle bag. This allowed them to leave the ruck sacks at the apartment.

As they were staying in Lagunas, Joe thought it would be interesting to visit Calamari. It is near the airport, and is a more upmarket than Lantanas and quieter. He took the lead, and told Kate to follow behind him keeping into the Kerb away from the busy traffic. They didn't have far to go, 3 miles, and they managed to arrive in twenty minutes. This wasn't too bad considering it was a bicycle they were using to get around

LAGUNAS

We stopped at the town called Lagunas it was three miles from Zanty. It consisted of one long street called Lagunas road, had great restaurants, bars and souvenir shops. Joe was hungry, and he made straight for one of them without looking at the prices. Kate reminded him they were on a budget and she directed him to another which was cheaper.

"What are you having?" she asked him.

"As its afternoon I'm going to have a pita." He replied.

They both had pita and shared giving them the choice to taste each other's, and they shared a bottle of the house wine. They chained their bikes up in the square.

They walked to the harbour and had a look at the boats that were moored and then went to see Saint Marks Square to see the church, which was famous for the interior inside, was lavished gold plating, extravagant chandeliers and plenty of marble.

They left the church and headed for the beach and paid for two sun beds. The sun beds were in front of the restaurant, and the waiter was standing with his tray waiting for them to order. Joe ordered two cola. When the waiter was out of hearing range he said to Kate.

"They expect you to buy as well as pay for your sun beds."

"Keep them on the table and don't buy any more." Kate answered and settled down to enjoying the sun.

They were on the beach about an hour when Joe had to go to the little boy's room. He was on his way back to Kate, when he recognized a face. It was the face of the man who was in the car this morning on the beach. Nee hid in an open door and watched to see where he would go. The other man appeared and they walked back down the beach.

"Kate get dressed we are leaving."

"Why?"

"Those men are here the men in the car the one's that I ran into this morning with the dog."

She quickly dressed and they went straight to unlock their bikes and headed back to Zanty.'

Joe didn't want to want to go out that evening and they had a drink at the bar.

Kate complained about the situation.

"It's not fair we have to tip toe around because of some goons."

Joe nodded but it didn't make Kate feel any better and she carried on sulking for the rest of the night.

"You are acting as though it was my fault." He said.

And she shrugged her shoulders and not saying it out loud for him to hear said,

"If you hadn't gone walking alone this morning we would not have been in this position." Back in the apartment at bed time they turned their backs on each other.

MAKING UP AFTER
A QUARREL

Joe was first to waken in the morning, Kate had sulked all night and at bed time she turned her back on him. He lay there waiting

For her to open her eyes. He edged his hands around her waist; she stirred and turned to face him.

He took her in his arms and he kissed her. She kissed him back, and they were friends again. Joe began to get amorous and Kate allowed him to fondle her breast and kissing her nipples. She felt herself being aroused and moved in closer, for him to take her. He wasn't quite ready and went on kissing her all over and when he was aroused they made passionate love. When it was over they lay in each other's arms for a few minutes before moving out of bed.

They planned what we were going doing later and decided to stay around the pool at the department. They would go to the Supermarket and buy some drinks, and have them on the balcony. Their apartment was almost in front of the pool and where so was the bar. They would have a drink at the apartment and see the entertainment that was going on at the bar.

***

A DAY IN BOUKA

Kate wakened and got out of bed. She quickly showered and dressed before waking Joe.

"Come on Joe, we are going out today," and she handed him a cup of tea.

"Where do you want to go today?" He asked.

"There's a little fishing harbour, and it has a small quiet beach and it's only fifteen minutes from here."

They decided to take a packed lunch, and Kate made breakfast while Joe shaved and showered.

They set off on the bikes towards Bouake, and when they arrived they looked around to see where they park the bikes. They found a place so they chained them up and set off to explore the fishing harbour.

It was a pleasant little village and the harbour was interesting. There seemed to be a lot going on, the fishermen were repairing nets and painting the sides of their fishing vessels. They sat by a tea shop for a little while, it looked on to the sea, it was so relaxing with the warmth of the sun on their face.

"Shall we head for the beach?"

"Why are you always in a rush?

I'm enjoying the sunshine and watching the fishermen." He gave in and they walked towards the beach.

Kate was excited when she first saw the beach.

"Wow look at the colour of the sand, and the crystal clear water, it's beautiful. Why is it so empty?"

"Who cares let's get on to it"

They soon discovered why the beach was quiet and the reason for it being so quiet. Was because the turtles are protected, and all water sports were banned. It was the season for laying their eggs.

They settled down to sun bathing and had a swim in the sea. But after a while Joe was bored, and he wanted to move on to where there was more activity going on. They decided to head back to Zanty.

Although Kate was enjoying the sun bathing and the warmth on her face she had to admit it was boring compared to Zanty. Where the beach was packed and music playing all day.

They arrived back at the hotel chained the bikes up grabbed some fresh towels and headed for the beach.

They arrived at the beach it was heaving with people and they both ran to get a spot by the disco and the bar.

"This is more like fun," said Joe and stripped down to his swimming shorts.

Kate warned him of the budget and he pulled a face.

"Let's not worry about the budget today we can have a quiet day tomorrow."

"We don't have to have any quiet days if we go to the supermarket and buy some drinks before we come to the beach

They agreed, after today, only to spend money on drinks at the bar in the evening.

The disco was in full blast, and was playing an old tune from the eighties and it was 'Bony M singing Brown girl in the rain.'

They were selling cocktails at the bar, and Joe came with two and handed one to Kate.

They took a sip, and laid the drinks down on the bar.

"Come on Joe let's dance?" And they danced letting their self be taking by the mood of the music.

MOVING ON TO RHOADS

Joe and Kate were due to move on and they were friendly with Christine, who owned the apartments they asked her which was the best way to get Rhodes. She came to the door with the Ferry time table. This was the best way to go around Greece.

They studied it and the time according to the time they had to leave the apartment. There was a ferry at two in the afternoon. It left from the harbour.

Christine advised them to go and book their passage across. At the harbour and booked their passage.

The office was just a small room with a window where you book your ticket.

"Now that's done let's go and have a drink and have some fun."

And Kate didn't need to be asked twice."

They were about to step out of the booking office when they walked straight into police with guns.

"Put your hands up and walk towards me?" said a huge policeman pointing a gun at them

"What are they doing?" Kate cried to Joe

But Joe could not answer he was being seized and bundled into a car. Kate was bundled into another one.

"Why are you taking us what have we done?"

No one answered her as she sat between two policemen.

They arrived at their destination and they were both pushed through a green door and put straight into a cell. Kate realized she was in jail, and started pleading with the policeman who was about to lock her up.

"Please don't lock me in what have I done?"

The same thing was happening to Joe only he recognised One of the men that was on the beach and he gave Joe a punch on the stomachs and he fell to the ground.

Where is your dog now, and he raised his foot to kick Joe.

"Hay that's enough" said another officer.

"What have I done, why are you locking me up."

But his pleading fell on deaf ears as they closed the door of the cell. It was a few hours later they let Kate go but were detaining Joe. He was being held as a suspected drug dealer.

"You're wrong" she said and pleaded with duty officer to let her see him. She was refused and she left the station and called a taxi to take her to the apartment.

Christine came straight to her and she contacted British Consul.

JOE MEETS THE BRITISH CONSUL

Joe was still in jail, and he was starting to worry about Kate. She hadn't been in touch with him since they released her, and police still hadn't told him why he was being held. He couldn't eat any of the breakfast they had given him, and now he was starting to feel hungry.

The British Consul arrived about eleven in the morning, and Kate arranged to meet him at the police station. The guards brought Joe out and Kate had to wait in the waiting room.

Joe was asked when the last time was in Greece.

"This is my first time in Greece."

"You have been in Greece several times." the Guard argued.

"I haven't been here in Greece" he protested looking at the consul who hadn't said a word yet."

He went on protesting his innocence and the Consul spoke for the first time.

"What makes you think he has been before?"

"We have been waiting for him to show his face in the country he gave us the slip a few months ago."

"You have been to this country several times?"

Joe couldn't believe what he was hearing and the Consul insisted that Joe have a break before answering any more questions.

Kate brought his passport with her to say when he came into the country.

Half an hour went by and the Joe was back into the room to face questions again. It seems he was supposed to be dealing drugs and this alarmed Joe.

He protested his innocence and answered their questions time and times the same question over and over.

He was eventually put back into his cell and the Consul promised he would do what he can for him.

Kate was upset she knew he was not the person they were looking for.

"When are you going to let him go she said sharply? "We will let him go when we are finished our enquiries and depending what we find we may keep him here."

Kate hung around outside the station, and the Consul directed her to a tea room.

"I will come and get you when I know what's going on."

Kate nodded at him and tears started to well up in her eyes and she made her way to the tea room.

When she entered the tea room she ordered a cup of coffee and she started to worry. Things looked bad for Joe.

A few hours later the Consul arrived with Joe behind him. Joe embraced Kate, he could see she had been weeping, and he reassured her everything was OK. The police had to admit that they had a case mistaken identity and let him free. They both had a lot of arranging to do; they were moving on to Rhodes in the morning.

***

CHANGING DESTINATION

When they arrived at the apartment Christine, who owned the apartments, came to the door to see if he was alright. Joe assured her that he was, and after hugging him she left.

They went to the cafe bar and had a meal and a few drinks after.

But they went home early. Joe went to the bedroom, and packed his belongings into his rucksack while Kate was painting her toe nails. She had packed most of hers while he was in jail. She went to join him in the bed room, he was fast asleep.

"Oh he is exhausted; I don't suppose he had much sleep being in a cell all night." She muttered and climbed into bed beside him.

In the morning they had breakfast in the dining room, before setting off to catch the ferry to take them to Rhodes. They left the apartment and the holiday feeling was back they had put the last two days events behind them.

They boarded the ferry liner, and as it was nice day, Joe managed to find two seats on the deck. The ferry was in dock for forty minutes before moving. They were enjoying the sunshine and the warmth on their faces. It was a pleasant journey and soon they were back on dry land. Unlike Zanty, where their hotel was booked, they had to find a place to live.

"Let's go to the main resort, and we will ask someone." He was already making his way to the Taxi rank as he was making this suggestion, and Kate followed behind like a lost sheep.

"Once in the cab Joe took the initiative to ask the cab driver."

"Do you know where we can book into hotel or apartments?"

"I can take you to a place where there are four hotels in the same area"

"Yes that would be fine."

The cab driver dropped them off. Melendez apartment's right in centre of a pretty little town called Lindros.

Here were plenty of bars and restaurants in the area.

Joe once again took the lead up to the reception desk.

"Have you any rooms?" he said in his Scottish accent

"A week maybe two" and the attendant nodded in agreement.

"But you must make up your mind in a couple of days

Making Up
After A Quarrel

If you're to stay two weeks." He was quick to say as he gave him the keys

Kate looked around and at once opened the door.

"What's the matter doing you not like the apartment?"

"It's alright we can sunbath on the beach,"

Joe looked to see why she was making this statement.

"Oh I see what you mean." The buildings were shadowing the pool

Area and it looked shabby.

"Worry tomorrow, let's has a shower and we can order a bottle of wine.

***

"No we are still getting married in Scotland, but not in the town we live in."

And he told her the whole story. And before they knew it the whole pub knew about their wedding plans. The drinks were flowing and they were a little tipsy by the end of the evening.

They would have to pack in the morning, but there was no hurry for them to give up their log cabin. It was paid for them to stay until the end of the week. They can catch the ferry any time tomorrow to go to the main resort, Crete.

***

Moving On To The Main Resort Crete

Kate was first to waken,

"Oh I'm starving what time it is?" "It's time for breakfast let's hurry or we will miss it."

The kitchen only catered for the group in the morning and in the evening. Kate and Joe would have to have breakfast with the group or go without.

They had breakfast and said goodbye to their friends and the instructor. They would be gone by the time the group came back to the centre.

They went back to the log cabin and started packing for their journey.

"Why don't we phone Mary and Rab and put our plans into motion?" said Joe,

They both went into the village and Kate called Mary.

"Hello answered Mary on the other end of the phone."

"It's me Kate,"

"Hi, Kate is you enjoying Greece?"

"Yes but I need you to listen," and she told her about the wedding plans.

"I can come alright but my mums bound to ask why." but she agreed to be there. Joe had made arrangements with Rab, and he also agreed to meet them at Gretna Green in Scotland.

"Mary says she thinks her Mother will get to know before she meets us?"

"Oh well we will just have to hope she doesn't." he said.

They finished their packing and made their way to the ferry. The crossing took twenty minutes and soon they were coming off it. Finding a hotel was a little more difficult, because it was the busy time of the year. They had to go into the back streets away from the beach to find one with a vacancy.

They took the keys from the receptionist and made their way to their room and were quite surprised to find it was a studio with a fully equipped kitchen. There was complimentary tea and coffee along with a bottle of water and a small half litre of fortified wine. Joe opened the door to the balcony; he was expecting to see a dingy pool judging from the look of the outside of the hotel.

He was in for a surprise all right. It was beautiful. No high rise buildings, a figure of eight styled pool, and an ornamental bridge going one side of the pool to the other.

They had recliner deck chairs as balcony furniture, and sat out on it and both fell asleep, their adventure holiday had caught up with them and drained their energy.

Kate awakened she looked around her and wondered where she was for a minute, and then she remembered she was in a different hotel. She looked across at and he was still asleep. She left him sleeping and she made her way to the kitchen to make a coffee.

Joe, awakened he was looking at her, and before he could make any amorous moves she said.

"I want to eat, and I'm all dressed up to go out."

He grinned at her and said, "You're a spoil sport," and he rose from the chair and went to get dressed.

"What you do want to do?" He called from the bathroom.

"Shall we get a takeaway and eat on the beach?" She called back to him. Kate was in charge of the budget, and now they planned to get married during their holiday they would need new outfits. She was looking forward to picking something nice. They had the money for this in their wedding funds.

They ate their take a ways and went to the Beach party. Kate was back on form at her Beech parties. The adventure course was fun but she was too tired by the end of the day to dance. She loved to dance and she seemed to make friends everywhere she went. Tomorrow she would go to buy the outfits for their wedding. But they still had six weeks to go, and they were going to enjoy every minute of it.

***

THE HOLIDAY CONTINUES

Joe arrived back at the apartment with a few groceries. Now that they planned to marry before returning home to Motherwell, they would have to be a little more careful with their money. Kate was finishing dressing herself.

"I bought some eggs, and some of those little bread rolls you like." he called to her.

He took the pan and filled it with water to poach the eggs put the rolls at a low gas under the grill to warm them.

They planned to have a day at the beach and relax but had to go to town first. She appeared still wearing her skimpy night wear. She had just finished ironing her shorts and as they were the colour white, she wasn't quite ready to wear them yet. He felt the urge to go to bed with her. He began to get aroused at the shape of her half naked body.

He made a move towards her and held her close to him, Kate reacted to his advances and held him close, but he said.

"I love you, and would like to take you to bed, but you are all nicely made up. Go and put some clothes on." She playfully urged him towards the bed, and then said,

"Oh all right I will go and finish dressing."

They ate breakfast and then caught the bus into town. They needed outfits to for to wear when they were to marry at Gretna Green. They also had to buy a suitcase to put them in, for traveling back. They only had back packing luggage.

They found a place that sold men and woman's clothing and Joe bought a blue suit and tan slip on shoes. It came to

picking Kate's outfit but she went on her own, while Joe
went to the cafe

Kate had seen an outfit in magazine a white trouser suit
and she would look for a look alike outfit. She managed to
find almost the same, and was pleased. She also purchased a
suitcase, and asked the girl in the shop to seal the outfit, up
and she made her way back to Joe.

They were now free to go to the beach for the rest of
the afternoon.

The Cats Out The Bag

After choosing their clothes for the wedding Joe and Kate went to the beach, Mary was to phone them tonight and Kate was anxious to know if Marry mother had guessed that she was getting married to Joe. Mary's mother had this knack of finding things out.

"I will get two sunbeds while you get the drinks in at the bar." Said Kate

She chose two sun beds far away from the bar," so they wouldn't be tempted to spend more money. The trip to the super market to buy an economy bottle of wine would save them a few pounds.

"I bought two beers and some lemonade, we can hold on to the glasses for the wine we bought"

A group of people were looking for people, to make two teams of players for volley ball, and water pool.

Joe volunteered for both of them. The games had taken quite a toll on their energy, and they hadn't realized how unfit they were.

"Whew, I'm glad that's over." Said Kate, and lay down to soak the sun up after drying herself when returning from the shower.

It was seven and she hoped Mary still managed to keep their secret of the wedding plans. It was time to phone home she was looking forward to hearing from Mary, and to tell her about her outfit, not too much detail though because Mary was a good looking girl and she didn't want the bridesmaid outshining her. She would tell her that she has a suit but not give any details.

Any way Joe will be in the phone box with me she thought to herself and I won't have to say anything

"Hello is that you Mary?"

"Yes" and Mary started tell Kate that her mother was suspicious when she bought her outfit and she had to tell her mum about the wedding. She met Kate's married sister at the bingo and she told her. Her married sister told her mother, and her mother told Joes mother.

"God she will be looking to see who's the parish priest is, and he will be calling on us at the hotel."

Mary gave a little laugh at his comment. Joe went on to say. "Keep your head down doesn't give her a chance to catch you on your own." He didn't get a chance to say anything more. Her father called for her to hang up the phone. On leaving the phone box Kate asked.

"What do you think are we still getting married?"

"Of course we are" he said and suddenly they had an excuse to go for a drink."

They were a little tipsy when they returned home and Joe began to give Kate a hard time because Mary let the cat out the bag to her mother. It led to a full blown argument and Kate ended sleeping in the bed and Joe slept on the sofa in the lounge, and in the morning he wakened before her and left the apartment. He went for a walk.

Kate wakened and she saw that he wasn't in the room he went to look for him, and she came across a little beach that she hadn't seen before, it was small but it had white sand, and she sat on the steps looking out to the sea. An elderly woman and her daughter were sitting also on the steps. She started a conversation with them. They told Kate how the elderly lady had come to this beach when the old King was alive. She was a young girl at the time, and she had come for to revisit the resort. Two hours had passed; she hadn't meant to stay so long.

"Serves him right he wanted to be on his own, so I have given him the space to do whatever he thinks that was so important to go walk about' s by himself." She said goodbye and began to walk back to the apartment.

She walked along the shore she didn't see the turning to come off the beach at the road which led up to her hotel. She was walking on her own. Joe her boy had stormed out of the apartment and left her. It was a silly not worth worrying about. A little problem that caused a flaming big quarrel she was wrapped up in her thoughts, and she didn't mean to stay out so long

Kate walked along the sand carrying her flip flops in her hand. Her mind was on the tiff she had with Joe and she kept walking on and on. She didn't see the sign about the Nature bathers, and she wandered into their territory.

It was really hot, and she realized she had been waking for some time. She sat down to cool her feet in the little pool of water by a rock. She stood up to walk back, and she nearly had a heart attack.

"Oh my God! What the hell is he playing at," and to her surprise. She heard a small boy saying.

"Come on Daddy we are waiting for you."

They were both naked and she looked away to avoid them looking at her. She started to walk away and there was another couple with no clothes on. An elderly couple about in there sixties, standing around a small beach tent. They bent down, both of them, they had folds and wrinkles. It wasn't' a pleasant sight. And she made to exit the site and back down the beach.

On the way down the beach she met Joe, and they went to the beach Bar. When she told him about her walk he howled and laughed at her escapade.

He was no longer in a mood; they walked back to the apartment together

"I'm sorry" said Joe, and went on to explain of how his mother would react at the news of the wedding.

"I know for sure that somehow she will be in touch with us before it happens. What about your parents."

"Oh they will say it all when I get home, but it will be too late by then so I don't think they will create too much unless when the priest turns up at your mothers, and she aske's him to go and see my parents."

"I can just see her do that." he said. "I think we should move on to the next resort and be ready for the return don't forget we have to spend a week or two in Gretna Green even with the special license."

They decided to go and see about the ferry tomorrow, for Corfu, They also booked their room in Zanty for a few days, at Christina's apartments. They were flying home from that part of Greece.

"Now that's all done, we have time to go and join the disco at the beach party."

MOVING ON TO CORFU

They looked around the room, to make sure there was anything that they had forgotten to pack, and when they were convinced that everything OK they closed the door. They said good bye to the girl on reception, and made their way to the harbour to board the ferry.

The trip across on the ferry to Corfu Wasn't long but it was pleasant. They strolled around the deck and went to the cafe and had cappuccino with cream on top, and then it was time to disembark.

They booked into the hotel, Shore Vitoria. It was right on the beach, and the view from the balcony looked on to the cliffs. It was dearer than the other hotels where they had stayed, but it was their last stop, except when they go back to Zanty. It was already paid for.

"Are you sure we can afford to stay here," said Kate.

"Stay here as in sleep sunbathe, but not drink or eat we will do that elsewhere, and we can eat in the apartment." The apartment was fully equipped. It had tea and coffee and mineral water on a daily basis that was already paid for, but any drinks you take from the Minnie bar, soft drinks or alcohol drinks were to be paid for at the end of your stay.

On the balcony you had room to walk around. It was not like the other ones they had vacated. Where you had only room for a table and chairs.

It had two sunbeds and a little sofa and two chairs.

"I will stay here and sunbathe, it's awesome." She said as she looked at the view. It looked on to the cliffs and the entrance to the beach.

"Let's unpack and get settled in." Kate said, but Joe had that look in his eye that longing look and she couldn't resist it. She loved him so much. He pulled her close to him pressing himself against her and giving her a thrill of excitement running through her body. He led her over to the bed. Undressing each other they had intimate pleasure and Kate didn't want this moment to stop they made passionate love. They lay with their arms around each other for a long time after. Until Joe said let's get dressed and see what the night life is like around here.

They dressed in evening wear, and had one drink at the bar inside the hotel, just to enjoy the fact that they were staying in a five star hotel.

The beech bars were the same others, and they expected to have fun here too. Joe went to the bar. Tonight they were out to enjoy themselves, they would economize tomorrow.

"Here you are cocktails, sex on the rocks." He said with a gleam in his eye, and Kate said.

"As long as it's in a glass"

"Well it is for now," and they both started to sway to the music and the mood of the night.

OUT AND ABOUT CORFU...

Kate awakened, Joe was still asleep she slipped out the bed and went and had a shower. She quickly dressed and started cooking breakfast. Sausages were in the pan the eggs were poached and the toast was on the table. "Joe, come on let's get going I have made the breakfast, and you promised to see the sights today."

"Oh my head what were we drinking?"

"Every vessel that could hold beer and cocktails." called Kate as she saw him disappear into the shower room.

He came to the table dressed in shorts, T shirt and trainers.

"You will have to change your shoes, have you forgotten we are hiring bikes today?" he said looking at Kate's feet. She was wearing flip flops.

They had breakfast and were heading out the door. They took from the Minnie bar a bottle of water for each of them. This was free along with as much coffee and tea they could drink in the day.

Everything else was to be paid for in the Minnie bar when they leave the hotel so they didn't take any of the other drinks from it.

The shop where they hired the bikes from was very helpful with their information of places to see on this part of the island and also there was the Island hopper ferry.

The shop where they were hiring the bikes from gave them a map and information on where to visit.

They pushed the bikes out of the shop. Joe was still studying the leaflet with the information where to visit in Corfu...

"Wow there is a theme park right on the way into our first visit to Glade Let's spends some time there. It has a water theme park and has large water slides."

Kate looked at the map and they decided they would call into it. They hopped on to their bikes and started the journey towards the theme park.

As they were approaching they could see some of the rides of the fair in the distance. They could also see a giant water slide.

"Look at the size of that slide, I can't wait to try that monster." said Joe

Kate looked apprehensive at it.

"Come on now no chickening out of any of the rides we try every one of them scary or not."

And she agreed, and she paid the entrance fee to enter the park.

THE THEME PARK

They were excited as they went into the park. With wrist band showing to say that they had paid for the rides for a full day, they headed to the water slides. There were plenty of rides but they decided to tackle the water slides first.

"Oh I don't know about this one, it's too high?" said Kate questioning her ability to have the nerve to go on it. Joe was already on the steps and starting to climb the stairs. It had a double slide.

"Come on you promised not to chicken out of the scary rides, look it has a double slide we can ride it together."

She joined him and they climbed the steps together. When they reached the top, they positioned themselves ready to come down the slide together.

"Ready One two three, and they both started to slide down it was very fast. Kate was screaming. She could see the water coming up to meet her.

Splash they hit the water like a ton of bricks and she felt herself sink to the bottom of the water and whoosh she came up to the top again. Joe instantly came up alongside her. They both laughed and exclaimed their excitement to each other, and made for the steps again to repeat the slide once more.

They went on to experience some of the water rides. One being like a roller coaster ride only you came down into the water creating a big splash at the end of the ride.

They had a break and had lunch. Kate had brought sandwiches and two pasta salads from the apartment, for their lunch. They had a beer to wash it down from the bar and sat outside in the sunshine. After lunch they went around the park, and repeated the rides several times. Finishing their day with a drink at the bar

They had an enjoyable day in the park.

They left the theme park and had time to browse around the resorts shopping centre. The shops were mostly gift shops and they bought a few to take home.

Tomorrow they planned to go to Athens on the Ferry Hopper to buy some wedding shoes. Kate had her white wedding outfit all wrapped up and out of sight from Joes eyes. She still believed in the tradition of not letting him see her outfit until she was getting married.

They checked their watches and it was three thirty in the afternoon. It would take forty minutes to get back to the hotel, and they decided it was time to go back.

"We can have a take away pizza, and collect some wine on the way to the beach party." said Joe. It would put the finishing touch to their day.

They went to their room to change for the beach party and as they collected their keys at the reception the receptionist handed Joe a note. It read

Sorry you were not at home when I came to see you. I will call back tomorrow if you can arrange a time convenient to seeing you. Father Gillespie of Saint Jude's parish of the Roman Catholic Church.

Joe looked at it, in amazement he couldn't believe his Mother would go to such lengths

Priest Is Coming To Visit

Joe looked at the note again, and threw it on to the dresser. Kate picked it up and looked at him.

"What now? Do you want to wait, and we will get married at home?"

"I didn't think that she would go as far as this, to send a priest to hunt me down?"

"She takes this religion a bit far, and how did she know we were here?" Said Kate, and still waiting on the answer to her first question.

"I'm not changing my mind to suit her. She will have her wedding when after we marry in the Registrar Office. And I will inform this so called Priest."

"I'm not in the mood any more to get dressed up. Let's just go the bar as we are." He said to Kate as he picked the keys up and made for the door.

They sat quietly Joe was getting drunk by the minute, and she began to feel uneasy. She had never seen him like this before, he suddenly broke the silence.

"Have you phoned home lately?"

"To my parents? No, my mother would be giving me the third degree, and asking all kinds of questions, but I have phoned Mary."

"Oh well that's where my mother getting her information from, it's not Mary's fault my mother would be giving Mary a hard time, until she retrieved the information she was after. She probably never gave Mary any option but to tell her."

"What do you want to do about the wedding and the priest?"

"What we will do is this. We shall move on to our next destination and instead of Mary and my best man joining us we can have two witnesses from the street in Gretna Green."

"We will have to keep a clear head if we tend to move on tomorrow. I don't see why we should be running away from here we haven't been here long and we have plans."

"Oh to hell I think you are right. I will wait and see what he has to say about it."

"Let's go home and make a night of it on the balcony with a few drinks, and after we can really make it worth the priest visit, by committing the sin of living together before marriage."

They left the bar laughing, and on the way back they picked up a couple of bottles of wine. They were planning to have raunchy night.

The Priest arrived on the time he had stated he would and Joe politely invited him into the room.

"Hello Joseph, what a strong and beautiful name you have after the Saint who raised the child Jesus. I have come because your mother has asked me to.

"Now what is the problem? Why do you want to marry in the registrar office?"

"I don't want to live without Kate, I can't go back to live or as I should say, we don't want to live with our parents in separate homes until we get married."

"But why in the registrar office?"

"We didn't plan any of this it has happened, and we both feel we can't go back to the lives we had, and if we had planned to marry, we would have brought the paper work we needed to be been married herc."

"How are you planning the wedding?" Joe found himself explaining his plans to the priest. After listening to Joe he said,

"If you don't object, I will arrange with the priest at your home town and explain your plans. He can arrange a blessing when you come home, because you will not be recognized as married in the eyes of the Catholic Church.

Joe walked with the Priest to the lift in the hotel. It was just outside the apartment door.

"Goodbye Father and thanks for coming."

"I wish I could have been more help to your Mother, but you have made your minds up and no matter what I say won't change anything."

"I will have a marriage blessing when I go home."

The lift appeared and Joe let out a sigh of relief. He didn't want to have another lecture from the priest. The priest entered the lift and Joe made his way to back the apartment.

He let himself in with his key and he took Kate in his arms and gave her a hug. He looked to see what her reaction was after the priest's visit.

"Do you think she will be satisfied now that the priest has been to see us" she said to Joe.

Oh I think she won't be happy until she forces us home, or she lands here in Greece."

We might as well go home and forget about this holiday if that is the case."

"No way".

"Can we get hold of the money in the wedding account?"

Why?

"There is one way of finding out let's go and visit the bank." You will know when I can and get access to the funds."

The Bank manager needed to see their passports and the cash card that held the money. Before lifting any money he explained to Kate what his plans were.

"We can go now to Gretna Green, get married, and come back here and finish our trip it can be our honey moon. I have already booked the special licence. What do you think?" She nodded in agreement

When Joe was asleep she crept out of the bed and had a look at her wedding suit

The Wedding Plans
Go Ahead

Joe and Kate went straight to the reception and booked a session on the computer. They emailed the registrar's office about the special license and were told they had a slot that had been cancelled and were given it. They were to marry in two days' time. Their next email was to the Airport to book the flight to Glasgow. They emailed Christina in Zanty to book the apartment where they first started their holiday. They had made arrangements to return to Zany before they went back home.

"Come on we will have to make any last minute shopping and he would make do with what he had. They had already bought their wedding outfits.

They were to marry at six o'clock in the evening and if they travel on the day before it would give them plenty of time to find a hotel and witnesses. They couldn't let the other two friends know because Joes mother would turn up at the wedding

They went back to the apartment and started packing their clothes to be ready to leave in the morning.

"Are you sure you will not be disappointed at not having a church wedding?" Joe asked,

"what's brought all this on, why are you asking this when we have made all the arrangements?" she said looking at him and wondering if he was having second thoughts. He reassured her he wasn't and she said she was happy.

I will still get to wear my wedding dress when we go to the blessing along with the reception. They were only getting married a little earlier than planned. Everything packed, and ready for the early morning flight. They went for a stroll and dropped into the Beach bar. They had a few dances when the disco started but they went home early. After a few drinks on the balcony they retired to bed. Joe held Kate very close but did not make any advances towards her, and he soon fell asleep.

In the morning they were surprised to see quite a few friends at the reception area to wish them luck. They paid the bill and said goodbye. They were now on their way to Scotland to be married.

Greta Green

After putting the cases through check in at the Airport, they had two hours to wait before their flight.

"Let's look at the shops, and I will buy you some perfume." Said Joe

"Oh yes please it can be your wedding present to me."

They entered the duty free and Kate picked some nice perfume, and Joe bought some after shave."

"Shall we get some for the witnesses?"

"No, I think they would prefer the money, I will have two envelopes with the money inside."

They strolled around the shops, and soon it was time for them to board the plane. Kate sat down she was all excited at the thought of their wedding. It seemed so romantic going to Greta Green. The Stewardess heard them talking and she asked them if they were really going to Greta Green. Kate and Joe told her about them not wanting to return to the lives they had after the back packing holiday.

They were given a complimentary bottle of champagne

The flight touched down at Glasgow, and when the finished going through passport checks collected their cases and made their way to the bus station to get the bus to Gretna Green. The journey was short and soon they were disembarking.

"Let's find a Taxi the driver will know which a decent hotel is,"

"Can you take us to a half decent hotel, not too expensive but one that we can tell the friends about?"

"Are you getting married?"

"Yes." they said in unity, and he drove them to a hotel within walking distance to the registrar's office.

The hotel was situated in pretty surroundings. The car drove pebbled driveway which led up to the reception door. It was called the Gable Hotel. Kate stayed in the while Joe went to see if there were any rooms vacant.

"I have a very nice room with a four poster bed." It was seventy five pounds for a double room. A full breakfast and evening meal was another twenty five pounds. He said he would take it and he went to the taxi to collect Kate.

"Shut your eyes," he said and led her into the room.

"Wow!" She said and ran over to the bed to test the bed. She looked around the rest of the room. A dressing table with a stool and brocade covers on the chair and a small settee."

We have time to freshen up before dinner; they both went to look at the bathroom, no bath a huge shower

"Plenty room in there to have some fun." he said to her and they both began to undress each other and they entered the shower together, and went through the motions of washing each other, kissing Kate on the lips, and caressing her small but firm breasts. Kate was aroused and holding him closely. He gently lifted her on to the bed, and together they made passionate love.

They lay together for a little while, before making a move to get dressed for dinner.

The three course meal was very good and worth the money. They both had steak and all the trimmings, and a choice of chips or potatoes.

Kate wanted to check to see if they had a hairdresser in the hotel. At the reception desk they informed her that they did have one and she made arrangements to have her hair styled before the wedding.

During the evening Kate began talking to a couple whose parents forbade them to marry and they were married in Gretna Green the day before. The girl befriended Kate, and agreed to be her witness her husband agreed to be Joe's witness. They had a few drinks with their new friends before they retired to their room.

They discussed the wedding, Kate wanted it to be traditional, and she didn't want Joe to see the outfit until he was at the registrar's office.

She would book two taxis one for Joe and one for herself. She would have to get some flower. She retired to her bed and she lay awake for a few moments and she was thinking tomorrow at this time I will be married.

The Wedding Day

Joe awoke first and moved from the bed, he showered and put some shorts and a tee shirt on. He started preparing breakfast. Boiled eggs and toast with coffee, He retrieved the champagne from the cupboard, poured two glasses, placed Kate's on a tray along with her breakfast, and went to waken her.

"Come on sleepy head it's our wedding day, champagne breakfast." She stirred and remembered she was in a lovely hotel in Gretna Green, and it was her wedding day.

They were not having breakfast at the hotel, because they planned to bring the witnesses, Julie and Bob, to the hotel for a wedding meal. He arranged with the hotel catering manager, to set it out as a wedding dinner. Two bottles of wine were ordered for the toast, and he was picking up a cake from the bakery. This was a surprise for Kate He wanted to make her wedding day special.

Kate went to the hair dresser and Julie went along with her, she had her hair up and held up with combs she bought from the hair dresser.

Going back to the hotel she sent Joe to Bob's room to get dressed and Julie and Kate had the bedroom to themselves, and she took her white trouser suit a brush cotton material, white shoes with a little heal she couldn't get too high a heel because they were both the same height. It was five O clock and she had to be there at five forty five. The taxi was booked for five forty. She dressed and looked a beautiful

Julie kept repeating this" You look beautiful." The taxi came and Julie and she stepped into it, she was on her way to married.

Joe couldn't take his eyes off, her she was so beautiful. They were called into the place where they were to be married and she took his arm and went with him and the service only took fifteen, minutes, and they were now husband and wife. The wedding group made their way back to the hotel, to have the wedding dinner. They cut the cake and toasted the couple.

At the end of the dinner they stayed a short while with Julie, and bob before retiring to their room. Joe carried Kate over the door and into the room because it's traditional, they closed the door.

***

Return To Greece For Their Honeymoon

Joe and Kate wakened almost at the same time,

"Do you need to go for breakfast?" he was playfully stroking her face he just wanted to lay in bed looking at his new wife.

"We have to go for breakfast, and we have to pack because we are going on our honeymoon." She rose from the bed and he came after her grabbing her playfully around the waist.

"No if we want to go to Greece, you will have to move out of that bed and start packing."

They were ready in half an hour, and on their way to the dining room. Joe was just in the mood for coffee and a glass of water. He didn't think he could eat a full breakfast. Kate had corn flakes and coffee. They finished, and they went to pack for their flight back to Greece.

As they boarded the plane she said to him,

"Are you happy Mr. Connor."

"Yes I'm happy Mrs Connor."

They settled in their seats to enjoy the flight.

It was two 'O' clock when they arrived in Greece, and three by the time they collected their luggage and through passport controller. Joe hailed a cab and they arrived at Christina's Apartment.

Christina had befriended them when they were in a spot of bother at the beginning of their holiday. She greeted the newlyweds and gave them a hug.

Welcome back Mr Mrs Connor, it's nice to see you again." She showed them to their room, they had booked for their return. She chatted to them for a little while and then she left the young couple alone.

The pool bar was just in front of their apartments and they decided to stay in tonight. Joe went across and bought two rounds of toasted sandwiches, and a bottle of wine. They sat on the balcony for a few hours before retiring to bed

Joe And Kate Are
On Holiday

Joe and Kate had one more duty to do and that was to let their parents know they were married. Kate knew how Joes Mother would take the news, not good but she didn't know how her parents would take the news. Her parents hadn't said anything even to Mary her friend.

"I know they must know, because your mother will have contacted mine."

"Oh let's go and phone now." Joe said.

Joe told his Mother on one phone and Kate used the phone kiosk next to the one Joe was using.

Didn't Take The News Very Well.
Kate came back with much the same news, and
My mother added
"I hope you have somewhere to live."

Joe was shocked at this news, he hadn't thought about where they would live, and Kate took for granted her mother would give them a room.

Oh let's not worry about it tonight we can work something out tomorrow, but Kate was upset, and thought her mother was being spiteful.

"She was giving us a room when my wedding plans were getting married in the church. What's the difference we are still married."

"Oh she might change her mind later; anyway it's my problem now I will sort it before we go home."

Rab and Mary were delighted when they heard their news and were looking forward to seeing them when they come home. They made their way to the Beach and they would announce their wedding. They are married now. They stopped at the shop on the way and collected their wine. Their intentions were to pay for one or two drinks over the bar.

The bar staff were pleased to see them back, and asked how they liked the other parts of Greece. Joe told them their story, and congratulations were given all round them. The disco started and they were away with the mod of the music, dancing to their favourite songs.

Childhood Memories

When we were children during the nineteen forties would get up to all sorts of mischief during the dark nights. And you didn't get prosecuted by the police like it is today. A neighbour wouldn't think twice in skelping your ear if they caught you doing something to their property. You didn't dare go home and say Mr Smith hit me for your Mother would demand to know why, and she would probably give you another skelp. It was on one of the dark nights that I became mischievous with my friends. Old man Robinson used to chase us from playing by the lamp post outside his door. Someone suggested that we should tie two doors together and knock on both doors. We chose his and the next door neighbour. The door handles were big iron knobs

We tied a skipping rope to both doors, knocked on the knocker, and ran. We would hide behind a hedge, and watch the performance of the occupants, of both doors, pulling against each other. Someone from one of the houses came from their back door to untie the ropes. They would look around to see if they could see the culprits who tied the doors but we were never caught.

We didn't see that it was wrong. We were children. It was only fun.

Another prank was to play in the dark and go raiding the gardens for those little neaps we called them. In Scotland, They were lovely and someone always had a pen knife to slice them. But luck run out on me. I was caught by the owner. He marched me to my grandmother, and she scolded me, but she never smacked me. I was put to bed and kept in for a week.

Today I love to grow things, and I shudder at the thought of some children or any other person who would tramp through my garden, and pull up my produce. Although it was the dark nights, we were all indoors by nine 'o'clock. We were children.

A Holiday At Butlins

I was on holiday with the clients from Stone House Day Centre for people with disabilities. I was a voluntary helper for Sadie who was married to John. Donald paid to go with me on this holiday.

After unloading the bus and settling our clients into their rooms. Donald and I went to join Sadie to find out which room we had.

"I have put you with Edith, Maureen, and May," she said.

"Oh no Not them, Donald likes a drink. They will gossip about me."

"I can't help it you need a double room, and that apartment has a double, a twin, and a single room." She remarked.

"Oh I groaned I can see this holiday is going to be great." I grumbled, and took the key from her. I made my way to the apartment.

I arrived at the apartment, and May let us in, and Edith gave us a cup of tea.

She remarked"

"I have to keep the workers sweet"

This gave Donald an opening for discussion.

"Molly is working. But I'm on holiday, and ladies I like a drink when I go out at night. So don't be alarmed if I'm a little tipsy when I come home..."

I joined in on the conversation at this point.

"You do know that he is not a helper, and that I have paid for his holiday,"

"Oh don't worry you will soon get roped into helping," Maureen remarked laughing.

Maureen was an ex school teacher before she had her disability and she once taught our children at the senior school.

I slipped to Sadie's apartment, leaving them all to get to know him.

John let me in and everyone seemed to gathered there,

"Do you need anything?"

"No not yet but if you can help me to dress before we go out. John usually does it, but it would be nice for a change to have a woman's touch."

I arranged to come back later, and went back to my apartment.

As the week went on we were all getting on fine.

In fact Donald was quite friendly with the ladies. He fetched them their paper in the morning, and he would do any other errands that they needed doing.

Maureen walked about pushing her wheel chair and when she was tired she would sit down and have a rest on it. She allowed him to push her to the dining room.

Sadie and John liked to go swimming in the morning at the fun pool. She sat in the pool, but John had his swim. I would join them in the pool and have some fun with them. When they had enough I would shower her, and by the time we came out it was lunch time.

After lunch she would go to her apartment, and a few of their friends would be gathered in their apartment.

This was my two hours off, and I spent my free time with my husband.

We had a busy time ahead of us in the evening I had to go to the bar for those who couldn't go themselves. The bar queue was about six deep. By the time two days had passed, Donald was fed up queuing for drinks. He gathered their money, and went to the cash and carry with John. We put it all in a large bag, and we did our own bar. Everyone was happy and Donald and had time to enjoy his holiday. I was surprised how he was blending in with the party and enjoying his holiday. He couldn't do enough to help them.

The young couple's next stop was to the night club, and I would to go with them.

We crawled into our bed at three O clocks, in the morning. Have a few hours' sleep, and then it would start again.

At the end of the holiday Donald says it was the best holiday he had ever had.

Their bodies may be lame, but the energy they had was ecstatic.

Hooray For Technology

I gained knowledge of this quality
Downloading

Skype at my daughter's request

I set up Skype and put it to the test.

Wow there in front of me

Were my daughter's 123

At first it was a sight to see

All My daughters in the lounge in front of me.

How did I ever forget?

The closeness to each other the three can be.

One quality they all share

Squabbling when together 123

And there they were in front of me
squabbling

But hooray for technology

I can switch them off and watch TV.

TENDER

Touch me when you're near

Endless love I have to give

Nearness to you sends electricity

Desire sets my body on fir
Ecstasy and passionate

Rendering your love

Birthday

Born many years ago
I have lived longer than some I have known
Remembering them well and sad they had to go
Tomorrow is mine I'm going to enjoy my day
Had a nice day and the family all came
Downed a few jars and they did the same
And now it's all over and I'm another year older
You only live once so be a little bolder

- 1 -

Eddie wandered around the office sorting files making work to keep from being bored.

"Oh if things don't pick up soon this will be another business going –to the wall." He muttered under his breath.

He turned his computer on to see if any clients had logged into his website.

He was just about to pick up the phone.

"I'm looking for Eddie Eagle is he in?"

A tall girl with auburn colour hair stood in front of him. She had legs all the way up to her arm pits.

Looking casually dressed, but smart he replied

"What can I do for you?" He held out his hand to greet her, and he pointed to a chair at the other side of the desk.

"My sister lives in Malta, and wants to come home, but because she is pregnant, a court order has been taken out to protect the birth, and he is insisting that she stays in Malta until she has the child, The reason for coming home to England is he is cheating on her."

She took a breath and added

"I haven't heard from her for months, and she writes regularly, and he has blocked my phone calls. I'm afraid for her safety"

"And You want me to investigate, It will be expensive, are you sure?"

"It doesn't matter, and she handed him one thousand lira, and she also paid for his flight.

"Let's get down to business what do you Know?"

She gave him a photo of the person her brother-in-law was seeing. He looked at the picture, and he almost whistled. She was a lovely looking blond and he could see why her brother in-law was tempted.

A few more details over a cup of tea and he was now booking his flight to Malta, and he booked to stay at the 'Draganora Hotel, in Saint George's Bay.' He had his first job and he was flying out tomorrow night.

Paula his wife was worried about Eddie going to abroad, but she knew he had to make a start somewhere.

"Be careful, and don't take unnecessary risks." She chided while she helped him to pack

Eagle's Way

Malta

Eddie kissed his wife as he was leaving her at the customs gate.

"I'll call you tonight," He called, as he was going through to passport control

Paula left and went straight to her car. She had never been on her own before and she hoped she wouldn't be scared living alone.

She was home in no time, and she had an idea she would call in at her mother's and ask if she would like to spend a few days with her.

She rang the bell and her mother answered it.

the airport. I came to ask if you would like to stay with me for a few days."

"I will pack an overnight bag."

She went into the kitchen and made tea, and her mother was getting ready.

At the airport, Eddie was settling into his seat on the plane. It was a three hour flight and he watched some TV, and When the drinks trolley came round he had a beer, and a whisky topped up with lemonade. He liked a little nip now and again, so he had another, and this gave him a happy feeling, as though he was going on holiday. He had to remind he was working, and not on a holiday. The plane landed smoothly and soon he was going through passport control.

The hotel was separated from all the other hotels and closed in from the road with an arched gate. The casino and a sports lido were in the same area.

The view from the window looked out to the gardens and the sea. He quickly unpacked and changed into shorts and a T shirt. The night was young and the resort was buzzing. He opened his bottle of scotch, a fine blend of Grouse whiskey and he poured himself a large measure. He took the keys from the dresser and left the hotel. The first stop was to one of the take-way's windows in the street, and ordered food and sat out on a bench and ate. Across the road was the Reef Bar, and he made his way to it. He noticed that the people in it were mostly tourists, and the Maltese people visited the open bars dotted around the vicinity. He will remember this when he was investigating tomorrow.

He was wakened in the morning by the birds chirping from the garden, and he looked at the clock. It was six thirty, and he went to the shower room. He showered and shaved and was ready to eat breakfast When the dining room opened. He was shown to a table. The waitress was just about to ask him for his order. A young lady arrived at the table.

"Do you mind if I join you?" And she was already pulling her chair out to join him.

"I will give you a moment sir, to get to know each other."

"I'm Eddie." He held out hand to greet his new dining room friend.

They chatted over breakfast, andhe had found out where she lived and most of her personal life in ten minutes. It was his police training. As the saying goes'

'Once a policeman always a policeman. 'He was finished breakfast, and was about to say goodbye.

"Do you mind if I join you as we seem to be on our own."

He was caught unaware and heard himself say.

"If you like."

And they both left the restaurant together, and they sat around the pool for a while. Eddie's attention turned to the job he was brought out here to do.

"I'm going I will see you later." And he went back to his apartment collected a map of the island, the photographs and set off. He took the local bus to the St Julians where his clients sister lived. Karen and John Martin lived in Josephs Street..

When he disembarked from the bus at the harbour, his first task was to the bar This was where he would gain most of his information, and would probably find john Martin. He entered the cafe bar and ordered a coffee.

He chatted with the girl that served him as though he was on holiday.

"Is this the main resort for night life? And what's on in the way of entertainment?"

"Oh no there is quite a lot of pubs here, but you want to go to paceVille, it's in St George's Bay"

He had just come from Pace-Ville, but he had to see Joseph Street where the Martins lived.

Eagle's Way

- 3 -

Eddie arrived at the hotel and went straight for his evening meal, and he took the same place as he had in the morning. A few minutes later his friend arrived. They had shared the same table at breakfast.

"Can I share with you?"

"Of course you can."

She pulled out her chair and sat and waited for the waiter to serve.

***

Eddie ordered a car to take him around the island, and to tail John and to find Karen.

Next morning he was up early and gave breakfast a miss. He was parked on the street, a safe distance away from john's house. He could watch him come and go.

John had Karen locked in an apartment in the attic and she was pleading with him to release her.

"You can let me out of here I will stay until the baby is born?"

"I know what you will do. Run, when my guard is down." He left her pleading on deaf ears, and he left the attic without saying another word.

Eddie followed him to Saint Paul's Bay. John pulled in at the parking bay and parked his car. Eddie quickly parked his car a little further from him, keeping a look out which direction he was heading. He was a few paces behind him. He turned into a bar, and Eddie followed him. It was quite busy, and he looked to see where John was. He spotted him he was ordering is pint, he was speaking with the bartender and seemed to be on good terms with him

"You're busy today?" The bartender nodded and turned to serve the next customer.

John lifted his pint went to play the slot machine. Eddie sat at the counter and ordered a pint. He looked around him and muttered.

"What a miserable room."

It was dark, and had one long bench where most of the customers sat, but he preferred to sit at one of the table's.

He joined John at the slot machines and engaged in conversation with him.

"How often do the machines pay out?"

John responded with a detailed explanation of how often the machines paid out.

Just as they were chatting, in walked the blond. Eddie spotted her right away from the ID in his wallet. She looked around the bar and smiled when she saw John

"Excuse me, I have just seen my friend." And he went to meet her. They both took a seat at the bar.

Eddie stayed close to them and managed to get a sandwich, when they ordered a meal. After their meal, they left the bar. Eddie was quickly on their heels following them in his car.

He followed them to Valletta, the capital of Malta.

After parking their car they went into a hotel Eddie walked into the hotel and nodded to John. He wouldn't be any the wiser as to what hotel he was staying at

He walked past the reception desk as though he knew where he was going. John looked at him.

"I think I'm being followed. Let's get out of her."

Eddie realized his cover was blown, and he decided he would try tomorrow.

Eagle's Way

- 4 -

He lay in bed late next morning. He decided to go to John's in the afternoon and nose around, and see if there is any sign of Karen. It was Sunday, and he strolled down to the phone box. He would phone and report how he was doing to Paula at the office, and phone his client. On his way back, to pick the car up he met his dining room frieSusan.

"Hello, haven't seen you around lately?"

Eddie, not wishing to disclose where he has been, answered.

"Oh I have been around."

She looked at the car.

"I wouldn't mind a run in your car?"

she said. He said he was busy today, but he would drop her off in Saint Julian's, and would pick her up again in a few hours. They drove off towards their destination.

"Eddie disclosed to her that he wasn't on holiday, but bent the truth a little."

"I work for a travel company, and I have business there today."

He dropped her off and at the high street stores, and arranged to meet her at five in the evening. He made his way to Joseph's Lane and parked the car where he had a view of the house. He had previous been to see a pet shop and bought some mild sleeping tablets for dogs. Wrapped up in a piece of meat. the bait for the dog lay ready beside him.

John came out of the house. Eddie ducked down low in the car, so he wouldn't see him when he drove past him. He took the meat with the sleeping tablets. He crossed over the road towards the gate and was surprised to see the blond sitting sunning herself on the Terra's. He crept back to the car, and he knew John must be coming back. He counted the windows of the house, and there were eleven. The window on top was a long narrow, and he thought he saw a movement of the curtain, but before he could investigate more John came round the corner. Eddie ducked down and waited until he passed.

It was a while before any movement was made at the apartment, almost an hour, and he paid close attention to the house. The blond went into the car and drove off leaving John. It looked as he was going to settle in for the night. He decided to leave and go and pick up his friend.

They drove back to the hotel and Eddie arranged to meet her at the dining room in an hour. They had a pleasant evening. A few drinks and one thing led to another. The few drinks they had relaxed them, and in Susan's apartment, Eddie suggested.

"Oh let's have a night cap."

He collected the bottle of scotch. The drinks made them relax, and he couldn't help himself. He leaned over to kiss her, and she kissed him back and began to unbuckle his belt from his trousers, and they both undressed each other, and ended up in bed together releasing their sexual urges.

He wakened and looked at Susan, and he felt guilty. He had cheated on Paula. He slipped out of the bed, and went along to his own room to sleep.

Eagle's Way

- 5 -

Next morning he was up early and driving towards Saint Julian's. There was little traffic on the road. He parked the car on a side street, and he took the carrier bag with hat and spectacles. He put them on and walked towards the gate.

inside the house, Karen was sleeping. Her captive had given her a sleeping pill. John and his mistress Kate were in bed, but not sleeping.

"I wish this was all over, said Kate."

"It won't be long another two months, and she will deliver the baby. Then we will get rid of her."

"What do you mean get rid of her?"

"Send her packing back to England."

What he didn't tell Kate that he was going to have her killed. He, Kate, and the baby were going to create a new life together away from Malta. He had already picked a spot to bury Karen. A pretty place with wild flowers, he at least owed her that. He thought,

"She won't know it's coming he had it all arranged."

Kate wanted a child so much, but couldn't have a child of her own. She was devastated when they told her at the clinic. She met john at a dance in the hospital where they both worked. He told her his wife no longer wanted to see him and went to live in the attic apartment. He said they had agreed that he should have the baby when born, and she was going back to England.

Outside Eddie waited for someone to appear at the door of the house. Kate appeared and went into her car and drove off. An hour later John appeared too wearing a hospital uniform.

"Now we are progressing, I can gather information on him."

He waited, and he followed the car keeping a safe distance from him, so he didn't suspect he was being followed. He must find out where Karen was.

"It looked as though John and Karen have split up." He said chasing after John's car. He drove to Saint Julian and parked up from John's house. He waited, and it wasn't long before John made an appearance. Eddie followed him to Silema, and when he parked the car. Eddie also parked. He followed him to a store, and when John went into the store He watched through the window. He was buying baby food, and clothes.

"Well well it won't be long before you lead me to her."

He came out of the store, and Eddie followed him, and was surprised when he returned to the house.

"She has been here all the time."

And took up his position to watch the house. He wondered why he hadn't seen Karen, and realized she was being held captive.

John appeared, and he had his uniform on. Eddie was aware he would be going to work.

From the car, he took the mild sedatives and the bread roll to entice the dog. He made his way towards the house and the dog began barking, but Eddie slipped into the grounds. He threw the dog the bread roll, keeping a safe

0distance the dog sniffed around the roll and then began to eat.

He made his way past the sleeping dog and round the back where it was more private. Taking his knife to loosen the catch of the window, and he climbed through into the house.

"She is not here." and he was going through each room. When he entered the top of the house, there were two sets of stairs, one set lead up to the top of the house the attic apartment and Eddie made his way up the attic stairs. He came to a door and tried the handle it was locked. He was about to walk away, and he heard a faint cry from inside. He listened to the door, and there was no sound.

"I must be losing my marbles."

He was about to go downstairs, and he decided to try the handle again, but he was stopped in his tracks, when he saw from the window John pull's up in the car. He knew he had to get out fast. He climbed back out the window and closed it behind him. He arrived safely at his car and drove off. At home, he was busy reflecting on his finding of the day. He was convinced that he heard someone in the room. He will go back and see, but not tomorrow, he thought they would be aware of the dog being drugged. He again thought perhaps he should go after the blond, and see if she would lead him to the affair they had. Up until

Now they had no proof.

Eagle's Way

- 6 -

He arrived outside Johns home.

"What the hell has happened here?"

He said in shock. The house was all boarded up and shutters closed, and the occupants had moved.

She must have been there, and he was mad with himself for not realizing that Karen must have been in the house, when he was there last night.

The dog being drugged must have alerted John. There was nothing he could do here, and he decided to go back to the hotel. The first thing he did was the phone the office to his wife, and he told her the story ending saying.

"I know where he works I will try and tail him again it means I'm going to be here a little longer."

"I will give the client your update, and we have other clients waiting." She said letting Eddie know he needs to be home.

At lunch time, he joined his friend in the restaurant and when he was chatting he had an Idea.

"Do you fancy joining we can go for a drive and take in some of the sights."

They finished their meal and left the restaurant. Mary went to her room and picked her handbag and cardigan from the wardrobe, and then they left the hotel.

"I have just one errand to do before we set off."

He drove to the car rental and had the car changed for a different model and colour. He made the excuse to Mary that the car was faulty. John was in the hospital, and was about to finish his shift and was Eddie was in the pub across from the hospital. He had given Mary a story that he may leave her for ten minutes.

"It's work doesn't ask what kind." and she nodded and waited while John went to his car, and Eddie chased after him.

John had no Idea he was being followed because Eddie was keeping well back behind him. He led him to a quiet area just outside Saint Pall's Bay. A secluded area with trees and land all around it. Eddie passed by as John went into the house. Kate came out to meet him.

"Gotcha." Said Eddie.

He went back to his friend and had a few drinks.

"What exactly do you do, this work of yours?"

"I'm a rep, and I have worked all over the island."

"You're behaving as though you have something to hide."

"Not quite, this is business mixed with pleasure."

They stayed at the pub until eight and Eddie realized John wasn't coming back to collect his girlfriend.

"Let's get you back to our hotel."

Back at Johns house Karen was in her first pains of labour, John said

"I will get the nurse."

"Karen picked up the words and had a glimmer of hope." She could pass the information to her that she was being held captive. She didn't know it was his girlfriend he was calling.

"Karen's in labour if you want this baby you better come now."

She finished phoning and thought,

"Why all this secrecy if she is willing to give John the baby?"

Eagle's Way

- 7 -

Karen was in the last stages of labour

"Where is this nurse?"

"She will be here" said John

Just then the bell rang, and Kate was at the door. John let her in.

"I'm not sure about this I can be struck off, let's get an ambulance, and send her to a hospital."

"It's too late for hospitals, she will have the baby here." Kate was still confused why he wanted her to have the baby at home.

"If you are convinced that she doesn't want the baby and is willing to hand the child over to you. Why is she have it here and risking the birth? There maybe complications."

He rushed her up to the room, Karen looked at Kate and said.

"Get her out of here I'm not having your mistress delivering my baby."

"I want to go to the hospital. You can't keep me captive here."

Kate looked at john in shock.

"What is she saying keeping her captive?"

At this moment, Karen let a scream out. It was too late to do anything, the baby was coming. Kate had no other option, but to deliver the baby. When it was over and Karen was so tired John took the baby from her and gave Karen a mild a sleeping draught.

"What shall we call him?" He said to Kate.

I don't know if I want to call him any name, "he is Karen's baby not mine."

"He will be yours I will see to that."

Kate left and said she would see him at work, and when Karen goes home to England. She didn't want to antagonize her anymore, and she certainly wasn't getting involved in any illegal plans, he has in mind.

Karen had been given the sleeping draught, and was sleeping

Next morning Eddie drove to Saint Paul's Bay. He went to the house where he followed John to. A sign 'To Let' was erected outside the premises. He had come to a dead end.

Karen wakening up and finding herself on a boat, let out a scream to try and alert attention, but it was impossible. The noise from the waves and the sea water hitting the sides of the high speed boat, just were too loud for anyone to hear.

John laughed at her efforts.

"Nobody will hear you, and If I were I would concentrates on making our son healthy."

"Why so you and your mistress can play happy families. It will not happen.

I fought you in court and I won, I have the right to leave and you can't hold me here. She screamed at him"

He wasn't listening, and her words were lost to the noise of the boat and the sea waves crashing against the sides of it.

Back in Malta Eddie is still trying to find John, in the hope he will lead him to Karen.

Eddie made enquiries around the area, pretending to be interested in property.

He first went to the bar, where he first followed John, to in Saint Julian's and he was talking to the bar man.

"I'm thinking of staying on for a while do you know of any properties for rent?"

"No but if I hear of any I will let you know." He paused and then said

"Where are you staying? I have a friend who has a place, but he is in Gozo for a while. He may rent his place out in Saint Paul's Bay."

"Oh no I was hoping to find one around here."

He didn't say any more. He just turned to the next customer. Eddie finished his pint and made his way out of the bar. His snooping paid off, and he was sure that the bar man's friend was John.

Eddie kept the room in the hotel but booked at the main holiday resort in Gozo.

Next day he and his car were driving on to the ferry for Gozo.

When he settled into his room in the hotel, he lay down for a rest.

"I will go to the bars around the resort tonight I may just run into John."

"Karen it's time to feed Tommy" John shook her on the shoulder. She was struggling to wake.

"Why am I so tired?"

"It's the baby, you are up during the night." he said. But the truth was he gave her a sleeping draught again to keep her disorientated, She looked around her and thought,

"Another derelict place."

The view from the window was just waste ground as though whoever bought the land planned to build on to it. She picked Tommy up and cradled him in her arms and said "I will have to find a way out of here."

Eagle's Way

- 8 -

Karen roamed the flat unlike the other she was not locked into a special room but she was locked in the house. With Bruno their Doberman dog to guard the home he was sure nobody would come near.

"I will get out of here if it's the last thing I do."

She picked Tommy out of his cradle and began to dress him. John had gone into town.

"Yes we will get out of here my precious."

She said to the baby playing with him as she was changing him.

Eddie spotted John coming out of multi storey car park his car park. He ducked down so not to be seen

"Ah the game is on again."

From his glove box in the car he took the hat and sun glasses, put them on, and mingled with the others going out of the car park. Keeping John in his sight.

He followed him to a bar with several other little bars in a row of each other.

Eddie took a seat in one of the other bars, and as the seats were all outdoors. He had a lovely view of him.

He was on the move again, and Eddie payed his bar bill and followed him back to the car park.

"Selfish Pig, he gets some fresh air and his pint, and he has Karen locked away somewhere." he muttered to himself.

They drove out of the car park and on to the main road. Eddie followed keeping well back so John didn't suspect he was being followed.

Karen looked around for something to whack John on the head, and she decided to try and loosen one of the slats shutters from the window shutters. She pulled at the panel until one came lose..

"Yes gotcha we will soon be out of here my pet."

She found a pair of Johns Jeans and a sweater, and quickly dressed.

"I have no clothes I can wear of my own so yours will have to do."

Eddie continued to follow john's car he drove through winding roads and away out of the tourist resort.

"He has her hidden well by the looks of this road." He thought.

Suddenly John turned into a drive way with no trespassing, and Eddie continued past the house, but kept an eye on the car through the back window. When John entered the house, he backed the car nearer, but out of sight.

Karen heard the car drive on to the gravel driveway. She rushed to pick her weapon up and stood behind the door. As he opened it and stepped into the room she brought the piece of wood down on his head, and down he dropped on to the floor. He was out cold. She picked the carrier bag he had in his hand and the baby and made a run for the door. Bruno was sleeping in the yard and saw Karen but he just let her go. He didn't see her as a threat.

She run out of the driveway, she had no idea which way to run and said.

"Please let him stay down and please don't let me have killed him."

Eddie saw Karen and called to her. She stopped in her tracks and was in doubt asking herself.

"Who is this is it one of Johns friends.?"

Eddie went to help her.

"Get into the car your sister has hired me to find you."

She jumped into the car, and Eddie drove away from the house.

She told him all about being held captive, and he said "I don't think he would let you away alive Karen. I think the police should be involved now." They drove the car to the nearest police station and instead of being concerned for Karen's safety they put both Eddie and Karen through a great ordeal of questioning, but eventually believed them and sent police to the premises, but there was no sign of John.

John came round from his whack on the head from Karen. He sat dazed before he realised what had happened to him.

"Bitch she whacked me on the head."

He knew she would go to the police so he gathered some clothes together and his passport. He would be able to take the ferry to Scissily. The ferry was due to leave in two hours' time. He may just be able to catch it. He boarded on to the ferry, and was asked no questions so far he was safe.

Kate was picked up by the police for questioning but was later released, because she didn't know Karen was being held captive. She helped with the delivering the baby and thought that Karen was rambling with the pain.

As she was leaving the station she felt sad. She believed John when he said he was to have custody of Tommy. Her eyes misted over and tears began to flow. "It looks as though I have lost them both."

Karen travelled back to England with Eddie and reunited with her sister.

John was eventually arrested in Sicily and brought back to Malta. Karen will return to Malta for his trial.

A NEW CASE

FOR

EAGLE'S WAY

Stitched
Up

A retire policeman was nicknamed Eddie the Eagle because he could spot if a suspect was guilty of the crime being investigated.

He set up his business in his garage in his home and was fitting some office furniture, the doorbell rang, an elderly lady entered the office. She was well dressed, and had short dark hair. He pulled out the chair for her to sit down.

'What can I do for you.' He asked.

She fumbled with her bag nervously before answering.

'I'm looking for my son he has been caught up in an incident and swears he is not connected with it, and fears he will be blamed

. 'Right stop there, and tell me what you know?' Eddie reached for a pen and a note book, and began jotting down notes. The account of her story was that her son was being stitched up for a crime he didn't do and it was his job to find him and prove he didn't do it.

Eddie studied the notes and the picture of Johnny Bell aged seventeen. He was invited to the party, and had just been released from prison a month before. He was enjoying the party when a crowd of youth's gate crashed it. The lad who held the party went to investigate the intruders and he was stabbed and somehow Johnny was holding the knife, but he didn't use it. During the scuffle it had been thrust into his hand, and Johnny panicked and ran from the scene of the crime, and his finger prints were all over the knife. Eddie picked a folder out from the filing cabinet and wrote the words. Stitched Up. A new case to be investigated.

Johnny Bell was well away from the Edinburgh and was sitting in an apartment in Holland. He only went out when necessary, he was keeping out of sight.

Eddie made his way in the morning to board a ferry bound for Holland. He had a pleasant journey and arrived on time. He was met by one of his old colleagues who previously booked him into a hotel. They had breakfast together and discussed the case. Eddie followed his friend's advice and they were to keep this from the police. Johnny would be persuaded to hand himself in if and when they find him, but Eddie had to find the evidence to prove him not guilty.

They searched the most popular tourist attractions but still there was no sign of Johnny and they gave up for the night. Tomorrow he would go back to the docks and see if there was any record of an address to where he might be staying. They rounded the evening off with a few pints at the pub.

Eddie to and his friend is at a dead end to where Johnny is hiding.

'I will have to leave you my friend and go and start my shift at the police station and my Boss will have my guts for garters if he knows that I'm working on your case.

Eddie and his friend parted, and he decided to hire a car, but in the back of his mind he thought that Johnny would be going around on foot. He hired the car anyway.

'Next stop breakfast.' Although it was nearer lunch time when he looked at his watch. He entered the cafe, looking around hoping to spot Johnny, but there was no sign of him. He sat out on the tires with his breakfast, and in the warm sunshine he ate heatedly

Johnny was laying low in a friend's house who he met in jail, Things were quiet, but he knew this would only be for a short time before his friend would ask him to do a job with him, and he needed to get away before this happened. He let out a sigh, and thought I seem to be getting deeper into trouble. He decided to go when his friend went out. He slipped his passport into his rucksack and prepared to leave at the first opportunity.

Next morning Robert suddenly said,

'Let's get out of here and have some fun?'.

Johnny groaned,

'I'm hiding.'

'Nobody knows your here.'

And Johnny decided to go with Robert

He took him to the Coffee house where they sell dope, and is legal to buy it in the coffee house. Robert thought he would play a trick on Johnny and purchased a pint of beer and two pieces of cake. He had no idea that the cake was laced with dope. Robert watched the effect that it was having on Johnny.

'Wow this is strong beer.' said Johnny

'Yep nothing but the best is sold here.' Robert replied, and ordered more and soon they were soon quite tipsy. They spent their time playing music and the slot machine. Johnny began to sober up.

'I have had enough for one day let's go home?'

And they played the bill and left the premises. Back at Roberts he felt safe again, and hooked his computer on to the TV to see the English news, and discovered they were on to him.

'You should go back and plead your innocent.' Remarked Robert.

How can I my finger prints are all over the knife.

He tried to remember the events of the night of the party and to who put the knife into his hand

Johnny crept out of Robert's apartment during the night, and although Robert seemed Supportive there was just something about him that wasn't right. He did long term jail sentences, and had the feeling that Robert was planning to do a job. The trips to the casino and always being around the area.

'He is up to something and I can't be involved, I'm in enough bother trying to clear my name without any more bother.

Eddie was coming out from the bus station He took the photo from his top pocket and looked at it.

'Well Johnny lad I hope I can find you before anyone from the law finds you.'

He entered the cafe in the bus station. And came face to face with Johnny. He couldn't believe his eyes, and he sat down beside him.

'Do you mind if I join you.' Johnny looked at him and began to panic, his mind racing did this person know him?

'I'm just leaving.' He heard himself say, and Eddie quickly added.

'I'm here on behalf of your mother, now you can run or hear what I have to say. Johnny looked at him disbelieving Eddie's statement.

'I have been hired by your mother to find out who has stitched you up. As long as you stay here the real culprit is sitting at home feeling pretty confident that you will go down for this and not him.'

Eddie ordered two coffee's and explained to Johnny that he was going to do his best to clear his name, but he would have to go back with him and turn himself in.

'You now have someone on your side, and I will do my best to get you bail,

Johnny travelled back to Edinburgh to turn himself in, but not before Eddie had every piece of information from him, about who was at the party, and who was near him when the scuffle took place when the youth was stabbed. Johnny visited his mother before handing himself over to the police. Eddie went along with him, but had no power to stop him from going back to jail, because of his recent release from prison, and he was still out on license. Eddie gave him his word he would continue with the case and prove him innocent. After leaving the Police Station, he arrived home to his wife and family to spend the evening.

Next day Eddie studied the information Johnny gave him and he had come across a few youths on the list, known to him when he was on the police force. The one he was sure that would be likely to be the culprit was known for being involved in similar cases, and he was almost sure that he was the culprit. He was known by the name of Teddy Boy Joe, and has the reputation of being a hard man.

Eddie put his jacket on, it was time to do some detecting and followed the lead Lanky gave him, and was as he suspected, the four lads that gate crashed the party were sticking together.

'If only the group would separate, so I can approach one of them," he muttered.

'Somebody must have a conscience for the stabbing?'

And he continued to trail them from a safe distance.

Lanky took over from him, and Eddie went down the local pub to meet his buddies on the police force to find out if they had any news on the case.

Johnny in jail waiting for news from Eddie, and he began to doubt that he would keep his word about finding the person who did the stabbing. He had dark mood swings, and put all his energy into going to the gym because he really wanted to hurt someone, and working on his boxing skills released his anger.

Eddie gathered the information they had on the case, the police had a suspect locked up and were sure they could get a conviction on him. He had a few pints with his friends, but didn't say much about the case,. He finished his pint and left the pub.

Lanky had observed the lads having a scuffle between themselves, and reported back to Eddie, and this was the lead Eddie was waiting for, and he thought, maybe one of them has a heart, and doesn't like carrying the guilt around, and when he next saw them together there were only three of them.

'A break through at last.' And he noticed fat boy Joe the teddy seemed to be the leader of the group, and the missing youth was a younger boy, than the rest.

Eddie decided to after him.

Saturday morning and Eddie is parked up on the corner of the street where Peter lives. He can see the front door of his home. It's the day of the Darby, and he is studying the horse racing page in his newspaper.

Peter too is studying the horses. He usually goes with his dad to the betting shop and then on for a pint at the local pub. He is apprehensive about going out, but his father would be expecting to go out with him.

'Oh well I suppose I better get ready.' He muttered, and made his way to the Shower room. He was almost ready when his dad called.

'Come on Peter are you nearly ready?'

He came out of his bedroom and joined his father.

Eddie seeing them leave followed on foot. The betting shop was full and they joined a few friends. Peter looked around and to see if fat Joe the Teddy was in the shop, but there was no sign of him and he began to relax.

Eddie blended in with the other customers, not too near Peter so he wouldn't be spotted observing them.. They placed their bets and left the shop to go into the pub across the road and again Eddie followed them. They sat together near the TV. With the big screen to watch the racing.

He took a seat a few tables away from them. Peter's dad noticed his son was quieter than usual,

'What's up with you? I've noticed you hanging around the house lately and you're not saying much today.'

'I'm alright I've not been feeling to well.'

His dad looked at him, but wasn't convinced of his of his explanation and turned back to the racing. Eddie waited patiently for Peter to go to the Gents, and he hadn't long to wait. Peter left the table, and he followed, but his dad noticed Eddie following his son. He arrived in the gents to see them speaking, and hearing part of the conversation when Eddie was accusing Peter of withholding evidence, and wrongly imprisoning an innocent man.

Peter's dad followed his son into the gents, and he witnesses Eddie accusing his son of sending an innocent man to jail.

'What's going on here? He asked.

'It's OK Dad.'

'No it's not OK who are you? And why are you questioning my son.'

I'm a private investigator.'

'What have you done? Peter.

'I haven't done anything but I'm involved in gate crashing a party and there was a stabbing.'

'If you turn yourself in, you will be given a lighter sentence which might keep you out of prison.'

'Give us until tomorrow?'

'If you won't tip off the others involved.' Peter nodded in agreement.

His dad went back to the racing, but phoned the family solicitor. They tried to enjoy the rest of the day but decided to go home and give the news to his mother.

On Sunday after dinner, Peter, his dad and the family solicitor went to the police station. Later on the same day Eddie handed over the recording of the conversation that had taken previously in the snooker hall. The rest of the group were rounded up by the police except Fat Joe the Teddy.

Fat Joe was almost home when he witnessed his brother being hand cuffed and being put into the police car, and jumping behind a wall waited to they left before entering his home.

'What do they want? He asked casually.

'His mother answered I don't know but they are asking after you.'

He didn't answer and went to his room, packed a bag, and left the house. Fat Joe the Teddy was on the run,.

The rest of the group were charged with holding evidence and affray. Peter was given probation, and Johnny was set free without conviction.

Back in his office, Eddie lifted out the folder marked 'Stitched Up' and wrote across it.

'Case Solved

Book 3

The Lighthouse

- 1 -

The story of the Lighthouse, the palace pronounced pails, by the Scottish people who lived in a miner's rows. Tommy McGee moved into one these houses, with his newly wedded wife, Bessie. Tommy was employed by the coal mining industry. He worked down the pits, underground digging coal.

Bessie worked in the same mine, but above ground.

"Let's lift you over the step."

He picked his bride up and carried her into their new home. A miner's house. If he left his job, in the pits, he had to vacate the premises. It was their wedding night. He put her down on the stone floor, leading into the two roomed house. One room had two chairs by a large fire place with a high mantle shelf.

Bessie had black leaded iron nest and a fire was made up ready to put a match to it. Her two brown leather chairs and dining suite looked real elegant. She had made two rag rugs,

and she placed one at the fire place, and one between the sideboard and the dining table.

The rugs would have to do until she could afford some wax-cloth. They had some supper before they retired to their wedding bed. A set in bed against the wall, with a curtain drawn across for privacy and, to hide the bed when not in use. He had the day off for his wedding, but he would be back down the pits in the morning.

Before putting the light out to join him, she looked around the room a surge of pride had come over her. This was hers and Tommy's house, and in another few months, she patted her belly, this little one would be joining them soon.

Before Tommy went to work, she knew how beneficial it was to have a nutritious breakfast before going down the pit.

She finished the tidying she looked around the house. Her house and a surge of pride and happiness came over her. Her next job was to tackle washing Tommy's working clothes, being down the pits everything you wore had coal dust in them. They had a boiler and a sink in the home, but these clothes would need a more and bigger wash tub. She had to take them to the steamy.

She looked at the Rote and discovered it was her turn today. She gathered her dirty linen and Tommy's working clothes, and she went to the steamy. She was apprehensive about meeting the other women.

"Hello I'm Bessie McGee, and I live in number 56."

"Jenny Crawford, I live in 37" offering her hand out to shake hands with Bessie..

"Just grab a tub any one will do, and this is where you draw the hot water. We have a dolly which you use to dump the clothes."

Jenny introduced Bessie to each person who came into the wash house and mixed in with the other women from the miner's row.

After a few months, Bessie was due to have her baby. She wondered if people would remember the date she was married, and count the months. They would know she was expecting before she was married. She pushed the thoughts from her mind. She was happy being married to Tommy. "It was her business, and no one Else's." She muttered and went on preparing the meal for Tommy coming in from work.

The Lighthouse

Baby Joe arrives

- 2 -

Bessie was busying herself preparing Tommy's tea, she cooked most days for him and he would be coming in from work in a few hours.

After being down the pit, she liked to have fresh clothes ready for him to put on.

She had only once gone down the pit when she worked in the mines, and she swore she would never like to experience it again. It wasn't only hard labour, the danger the men were in was unbelievable. Trams carrying coal swishing by and the miners had to be alert and know what they were doing, and with only a little lamp attached to their helmet for them to see. It was an extremely dark and dismal job he had, and she sympathized with him one hundred per cent. It was only a year ago when they stopped children from working down the pit. They are allowed to work at the top but not until they are thirteen.

Bessie thought about her little one inside, and she said. "This little one won't go down any pit. Bessie felt this trickle of warm liquids trickle down her leg." She looked down to see a puddle form on the floor.

"Oh! It must be time for the baby to come?" And she went to seek help from her
friend Sadie.

Sadie put Bessie to bed, and she sent for the mid wife. Her name was Lizzie, and she attended to Bessie for a few hours before the delivery of the baby. Lazier, had delivered most of the babies in the minors row. Joseph McGee had arrived and was howling, and letting everyone know he was here.

Tommy was given the news when he surfaced to the top of the pit, and he hurried home to his wife and new son.

Bessie stayed in bed. Tommy was home, but she had to get out of bed the next day, when he returned to work. The mine bosses didn't think it was serious enough to take time off.

Bessie had to get up whether she felt week or not. She had a terrible time delivering the baby. Sadie came and gave her a helping hand for a few hours.

Living in the palace

- 3 -

Bessie went to visit her parents on a Wednesday and had tea with her. She took Joe in the pram, and she would take a few groceries to them. It gave them time to play with their grandson.

She was quite well off; the miners had considerable wages and plenty of coal to keep them warm. Tommy would take a bag of coal to them, but not too often. He stressed the fact that his job was dangerous, and he had to work hard for his earnings. Bedside's dad was ill and couldn't work so she insisted that she took some groceries, especially fresh eggs.

In the Palace, the women when washing would put their washing out on a shared green in front of the houses, not at the back like most premises On a Monday in the mines row, everyone seemed to be in competition, to see whose washing was the cleanest. There was washing in every green and, Bessie had to put her nappies out quick in the morning, or her neighbour would take up all the space on the green.

It was two years later Bessie had a little girl, and she called her Kate. Tommy said that was all the family he wanted, and Bessie agreed with him two was the ideal family. And they could give more to their children this was the best way to get on. Life was suitable for the McGee family.

Joe grew up and went into the merchant Navy. Kate was due to leave school, but Bessie insisted she stay on at school and do her Scottish Highers exams she wanted a better life for Kate. She hoped she would go into teaching, or some other professional job.

It was her day for the steamy, and women were joking with each other.

A repeated horn sound was blasting and letting people know there was an accident.

Kate was panic stricken, and Sissy M.C. bride was already pulling off the rubber apron she wore in the steamy.

"Come on let's go and find out what has happened."

She had been through this before she didn't tell Kate it must be serious for to blast the horn.

They joined the other women making their way to the mine. They were lost in their own thoughts and each hoping it was someone else's husband or son.

Bessie's tragedy

- 4 -

When they reached the mine they were told there was an explosion and some of the section where Tommy worked had collapsed on top of the men. They waited for news, and someone at last said.

They are coming up, and everyone moved nearer. The men were coming out of the cage.

She couldn't see Tommy, they were bringing someone a stretcher it was covered. Bessie said I can't see Tommy. One of the inferiors made to comfort her.

"oh God its Tommy." "And she collapsed into a heap on to the ground."

She was brought round with smelling salts, the neighbours were around Bessie.

"Please say it's not Tommy?"

She asked the women who were with her from the steamy. They looked at her and one of the women said.

I'm sorry, but it is Tommy, and she put her arm around Bessie. Let's get you home and the helped Bessie to her feet.

One of the women arranged to get Joe home from the merchant navy, and another went to meet Kate from school.

The Doctor came to the house and gave Bessie a sedative.

"You will have to be brave Kate for your mother." "He said to her." "Joe is on his way home." she replied,

And Kate thought how she could be brave. She was hurting too. Joe came in late that evening. They hugged each other sharing their grief.

The next few days were hard to get through but the worst was yet to come

Joe did all the arrangements with the preparing for his father's funeral. Bessie had things on her mind. Kate would be homeless. Joe would be alright, he could go back to sea.

Kate looked at her mother in deep thought.

"It will be all right mum, let's not worry about anything until after the funeral."

Kate stirred from her thoughts, and she agreed there is no use dwelling on the situation.

She would try and put the problem away until the funeral.

Sadie next door came and sat with her while Kate and Joe went to the undertaker to pick the coffin. Bessie had chosen it from a book, and they only had to finalize the choice.

There was a massive turn out at Tommy McGee's funeral, all the neighbours and men from the pit., Tommy was cremated, and his ashes were put in the garden of remembrance. Only a few selected friends and family were invited back to the house for refreshments.

The neighbours would miss the McGee family it was a well-known fact that if you didn't work down the mine you lose your house. No matter what the circumstances.

Bessie waited until everyone had gone before she approached the subject. Joe told his mother to do nothing until she received a letter of eviction. This would give him time to see if he could find somewhere for them to live. He was going back to join his ship, and he was going to see if they could do anything for them, at the recruitment office.

The recruitment office did manage to find him a job was a Lighthouse Keeper.

It was in Burnt Island in, Foreshore, Scotland.

He didn't want to leave the job he had, but it came with a cottage, and he had to provide a home for his Mother and sister. He accepted it gracefully.

Bessie eventually received the eviction notice, and she started planning her move to Burnt Island. Before she moved she went around the miners rows to her neighbours and friends to say goodbye.

They both took one last look around the house that Tommy brought her to on their wedding night. A tear escaped from her eyes. She quickly dried it before Kate saw her she had to be brave for Kate's sake. They closed the door and left the key at the office, and went to the train station.

Burnt Island

- 5 -

Joe made his way down the gang way for the last time; He was leaving the Merchant Navy. He was catching the train to take him to Burnt Island. Before he was to board the train, he had gone and had some breakfast and bought a loaf of bread and cheese this would do him for supper tonight.

On arrival, he went straight to the office to pick up the keys of the cottage. He approached a worker painting a boat in the yard.

"Where can I find Mr? Campbell?"

"Just go up those steps, and his office is just inside the door."

He made his way up the steps and introduced himself to the Mr Campbell. He gave him his work Rote to start a week later. He had to stay on the lighthouse on shifts, for two weeks on and two weeks off. He took the keys of the cottage, and made his way to the cottage

Joe said goodbye, and arranged to be at the office in two weeks' time to start his new job. Mr Campbell is the skipper, who would ferry him to the lighthouse.

He took the keys of the cottage and the written instructions how to get to it. It was just a ten minute walk to it. He hoist his kit bag up on his shoulder and began walking along the sea front.

The tide was in, and the waves were crashing against the sea wall. The sun was shining and the air felt fresh. The guest houses across the road all had signs saying full on them.

This was a clear sign of being a delightful place he thought a more pleasant house than the pit house. He wondered how his mother would feel about leaving the pit house. His mother lived in the house since she was married. He hoped she would be all right living here. The sign said Petty cure Bay and he looked for the cottage.

"The cottage should be here on the right." He mumbled. He turned the corner, and it was in front of him.

Number 92 Putty cure Bay Road, a broad smile spread across Joe's face. He was pleasantly surprised. A front garden, which had a white picket fence around it. He took the key and turned the lock and entered the cottage.

The first room was the lounge with a set in bed against the wall, a large range to heat the room... The range had two ovens. On the hearth of the fire, there was some logs, that had been left to dry. The previous keeper had left the fire made up ready to light. A door led to the kitchen which was small. It had a boiler in the corner, and two sinks one was covered with a board which served as a draining board, when the sink was not in use.

Another door led upstairs to the bedrooms and to his surprise a room with a bath and a water closet.

"No more running down to the toilet in the yard during the night as he had done in the last house."

Said Joe as he turned to go back down stairs.

He laid his sleeping bag on the set in bed took the food and made some bread and cheese, lit the fire and settled in for the night. His mother and sister were arriving on the six o'clock train tomorrow night. The furniture from the last house was arriving in the morning.

The family is reunited.

Joe was up early, he went to the bathroom, and he had a wash at the sink. There wasn't enough hot water for a bath. But he enjoyed having his wash in privacy

He was used to washing and shaving in the kitchen at the pit house. This made a significant change; no one would be entering the bathroom, like they did in the kitchen. He was to wait for the furniture to arrive. It was due to arrive, half an hours' time, so he ate the rest of the bread and cheese for Breakfast.

The men had arrived, and he helped them to unload it. He placed the furniture to where he his mother would like it, and creating a homely feeling for them to come home to.

When the removal men left, he went for some shopping, because the shops will be closed when his mother and sister arrives.

He stood on the platform at the station, and waited impatiently he worried about what his mother would be like. How she would be feeling. It was unlucky enough that she lost his father but to lose the home that she lived in all her married life. She would be feeling miserable.

The train came, and he ran to meet them, it was a month since his father died and after the funeral, he had to return to his ship.

"Mum how is you?" He put his arms around her to comfort her not leaving Kate out he drew her to him and gave her a reassuring hug.

"Oh mum you should see the cottage you will love it."

"Well the air will be cleaner." She replied, and she handed the suit case and a sewing machine which Tommy bought her, so she could work at home, Instead of going out to work. They made their way to the tram stop, and waited for it to arrive.

Kate was excited when she saw the cottage.

"Oh mum it's lovely," and Bessie nodded her head, but she thought it's still a tied house. If Joe loses his job, they will be back on the street with no home.

She made up her mind to try and get a rented house not attached to Joe's job.

Bessie was pleased with Joe's work how he had placed the furniture. She went to the sink and filled a kettle and placed it on the range. Those ovens will come in handy she thought. Joe noticed a faint glimmer of a smile on her face. She was also pleased that it had a bathroom and a water closet.

She started supper, and when it was over she sat at her sewing machine and made a pair of curtains go in front of the sink, to make it neat she could store her saucepans under there.

They sat chatting about Tommy most of the night. Bessie felt her eyes start to well up and the tears started to flow. She quickly dried them and said.

"I will miss your dad, but I have turned another corner, and I will have to get on with it." They decided to go to bed. Kate went up to her room. Joe followed a few minutes after to his room, leaving Bessie, to put the fire guard up and lock the door. Bessie chose the set in bed; she was used to sleeping in the one at the miner's row at the pits. Before she went to sleep she spoke to Tommy,

"Well Tommy, tomorrow I will have to start a new chapter in my life without you"

A New Beginning

A new day, Bessie thought, time to move on. She opened the curtains, what a view the sea, the tide was far out. You would have to walk quite a distance if you wanted to go for a paddle or to swim. The beach was deserted, unlike the resort, Burnt Island ten minutes' walk from the cottage, which was full of day trippers and holiday makers.

"A different view to what we have been used to." She said to Kate who had just come down stairs from her bedroom.

"It's beautiful, but I will miss my friends."

"Oh you will make new friends, and the friends you have left behind you can

Invite them down for a holiday."

Kate brightened up at the thought of seeing her friends again, she would write a letter to her best friend, and she can pass the news to the others

Bessie started to cook breakfast, Joe appeared washed shaved and dressed.

"It's Sunday Mum, I have a week before I start my new job.so let's explore the island."

Bessie quickly tidied around the house and went upstairs to have a wash and get dressed.

She chose a blue flowered dress, and put white sandals on. She took a white cardigan, in her shopping bag, in case it turned chilly. She was ready to go out.

They walked along the back road, until they came to the promenade, they walked along it looking at the day trippers and holiday makers.

"Do you want to sit on a deckchair on the beach?" Joe asked his mum.

"No not today, let's find our way around first." she replied.

They walked on, and Bessie suggested that they had tea in the cafe across the road.

They ordered tea and Kate had a fruit juice. Kate noticed a sign on the door saying STAF WANTED, and she went to the counter. She explained about Joe's job, and this seemed to satisfy the owner. Bessie was given the job, and she was to start the same day as Joe was to start his new job. The owner gave her some information on the schools, and she decided to register Kate on Monday.

They made their way to the main shopping centre and found the Post Office. It was inside the Town Hall, it was closed, because it was Sunday, but they now knew where to come for stamps when they needed them.

Before going home they went around the fairground Joe enticed her on to the waltzed, and she enjoyed the ride. Joe and Kate went on some other rides while Bessie stood at the side bar and watched them. She had a quiet thought to herself. If only Tommy were here, a tear tricked down her face, and she wiped it before the children could see her cry. As they walked back to the cottage they had some fish and chips from one of the many chip shops along the promenade.

"Where is the lighthouse?" Kate asked Joe.

"It's the other side of the Island you will have to go into King Horn to see it. It's in the other direction from the cottage. If you would like to go and see it, we can go tomorrow"

And they agreed to go into Kinghorn to see the lighthouse tomorrow.

The view of the lighthouse

On Monday Bessie went to the school to enrol Kate, she would leave at Easter next term, but Bessie wanted her to stay on and do her Scottish Highers exams. She had to travel on the bus to Kirkcaldy which is just the next town to Burnt Island. It was only fifteen minutes on the tram. The new term started the week after Bessie started work.

"I will be all right, she said. I will busy myself down town, and I can call into see you at the cafe."

With this in mind Bessie relaxed a little. After lunch they went for a walk to look at the lighthouse Joe was to work on. The lighthouse was in Kinghorn, but the job was based in Burnt Island. They had to walk in the opposite direction from Petty cur Bay. The walk only took them ten minutes to reach the town. It was a nice clean little town, with a sandy beach. Joe took them to the point where he thought was best to view the lighthouse.

It stood there in the water looking dark and gloomy,

"It looks better at night it is all lit up." said Joe

"It's quite far out?" said Kate putting a penny in to see through the binoculars on the prom.

"Yes that's why we have to travel out in Mr Campbell boat" replied Joe.

"I wasn't sure about the keeper job but as time goes on I'm getting used to the idea." He said to his mum.

"It won't be for ever, I fully intend to look for a rented house without it being tied to you job, and at least you will have the choice to where you will want work."

Bessie spied a cafe and ushered them across the road to it.

The cafe faced on to the beach, and they could see all that was going on. The sea was calm and the sunshine was glinting on the water making rainbow colours on the waves.

It was peaceful and it was like they were having a little holiday. Joe raced across to the beach with Kate and they were having fun in the water, whilst Bessie ordered another tea and watched them from her table.

The rest of the week flew by and soon it was time for Bessie to start in the cafe and Joe to start his two week shift living in on the lighthouse.

He arrived at the boat yard bright and early. Mr Campbell introduced Joe to Tommy Perry, the other keeper that was to be on duty with him.

"There are always two keepers on duty at the lighthouse."

Joe was relieved at this news; he had been worrying about being on duty alone.

Mr Campbell and the two keepers loaded the boat with enough provisions to last two weeks; He also did a trip out with fresh meat to the lighthouse once a week.

They were loaded and on their way, Joe was about to experience the duties of the lighthouse keeper.

Settling to into the new jobs

Bessie arrived at the cafe at nine in the m

The cafe doesn't get busy until about ten, so you can wash up while you are waiting. Bessie took the apron from her shopping bag, wrapped it around her, and she started washing the dishes. At ten the shop started to fill up with shoppers and she was busy taking orders for the morning. A two o'clock she managed to have ten minutes break. Peggy came over with another cup of tea for her and a sausage roll.

"On the house, it's been so busy out there, and you have proved you're worth having as a worker." Bessie thanked her.

At The lighthouse Joe climbed the spiral stairs to the lounge, Tommy put the kettle to boil.

"I always start with a cup of tea; after we have had our tea I will show you the routine and show you around the place." Tommy was a cheery and fun person. He had only known him for an hour, and he already felt he knew him all his life.

The room was quite big for a lighthouse, Joe was surprised. The two chairs were not new but very comfortable, it had a cabinet which held the crockery and food. The range was black with red tiles on each side of the fire.

The upstairs rooms were bedrooms two and the last floor was the lamp room. Where the lamps continued to light up the sea, and warn the ships of the dangerous rocks that surround the coast.

"I hope you know how to cook because you have to take your turn at it." Tommy.

"Don't worry I can boil an egg and do soldiers." Joe replied.

Tommy took him to the lamp room to show him the routine of how to keep the lamps running smoothly. Joe was asking all sorts about the light house, how it was built and what materials and the history of it. Tommy could only tell him a little of the history. When his fourteen days were over and he had two week off. He would go to the library and read about them. He would sit and tell his mother what it was like to work on it.

Bessie decided to take in sewing as well as the cafe job, she was determined to save to afford another rented house, and get away from the tied cottage.

Kate was offered a weekend job at the cafe, and she was able to buy some of her own clothes.

She sometimes went to the cafe, and worked Friday night, instead of the Saturday.

"Do you want to climb Bin Hill?" Joe asked Kate.

"Yes if you like." she replied and made her way to get ready to go with him.

They dressed in tracksuits and a warm hat and gloves.

They made their way towards Burnt Island to the hill. Bin Hill is the highest point in Burnt Island and you can almost see Edinburgh the capital of Scotland.

At the bottom Joe took the lead climbing his way up. Kate came behind him, puffing and panting and out of breath. Joe waited at the top for her to join him. They sat on the grass to catch their breath, before viewing the scenery all around the Island.

"Look Kate you can see the Forth Bridge, this was the railway bridge that joined Edinburgh to Fife." Kate looked at the scenery; she could see every point of the Island from here. Joe pointed out the lighthouse. It looked spooky in the daylight. A dark grey building it looked gloomy.

Kate settles at school

- 9 -

It was Kate's first day at school; this was the top band before she would join the six formers next year. She loved school but she was apprehensive about the new school. She didn't know anyone yet.

"Oh well no point in worrying I'm here now."

She pushed the door open, it led to a long corridor, the smell of polish caught the back of her throat, and she gave a slight cough. The head teacher's room was in front of her and she hesitated, before she knocked on the door. The secretary gave her a time table, and directions to her first class. English. Mr McLaughlin's. She opened the door, everyone in the room turned to look at her.

"Quickly take a seat and we will do the introductions later."

Kate found a seat next to a girl, she move up to give her more room.

At break the girl sitting next to her introduced herself.

"Hello I'm Annie, would you like to join me during the break?" Kate shook her hand. She introduced herself and followed Annie to the school canteen. Annie was doing the same subjects as Kate so they shared the same desk, for the rest of the day. At the end of the day she parted company to catch her bus home, agreeing to meet her in the cloakrooms in the morning.

She had made a friend, and the school wasn't too bad now that she had the first day over.

She boarded her bus to take her to Burnt Island. She went straight home. Mum would be at home, she finished early today.

Bessie had the evening meal ready, and she put them on the table. Joe was in the lighthouse, so there was only the two of them.

"How did it go?" she asked anxious to hear what she had to say.

"Oh all right, everyone was friendly and the lessons were okay." Bessie didn't ask any more questions and Kate didn't offer any more information.

They ate their dinner in silence, Bessie with her thoughts about her dead husband, and as for Kate, she would tell her more about her day when she was ready.

She cleared the table, and after washing the dishes, she took her sewing machine from the cupboard. She had an order to make two dresses for her boss in cafe.

Later she would do some baking for Joe; Mr Campbell was going to take it to Joe on the Lighthouse

Tommy was making the dinner when they heard the motor of the boat arriving,

"Mr Campbell," they both said at the same time, and made their way down to the lower floor to help unload. He handed over the food and fresh meat, bottled water and some magazines and the baking tin with the cake and scones from Joe's mum.

Tommy tossed the football magazine to Joe. He had it on order each month.

He looked at the motor bike one that was on order for him. Joe was opening the baking tin.

"Plenty of cakes for us later."

"Well the dinner is ready so let's eat it before it gets cold." Tommy said and he started dishing it out on to the plates. The lamps needed attention and Joe went to the lamp room. Tommy finished tidying round before joining him.

The daily routine went on as normal. It was time to change keepers they had two weeks off now.

Bessie had saved enough to put her plan into action. She now had enough for a rented house, that wasn't attached to Joe's Job.

She had put her name down for rented accommodation. A letter arrived in the morning post. It was from the landlord who owned property. A three bedroom tersest house has come available in Kinghorn. Bessie was all excited she had never had a house that wasn't tied. She thought about Tommy her dead husband and how they had to move because they lived in the tied house belonging to the pit.

Joe was a little disappointed about her wishing to move.

"I like it here" he said,

"I like it too, but if anything should happen to you we would be back on the streets. I'm looking at the house and if I like it I'm moving."

He just looked and he knew she was right, but he felt good knowing he provided a house for them.

Bessie and Joe went to view the house.it was modern, someone lived above them, they had an inside toilet and a kitchen with a boiler to boil clothes. An extra bedroom and a garden. She was happy with the term and signed to rent the property.

It took three days for Bessie to move, Peggy gave her holidays, so she could move. Tommy was due to go back to the Lighthouse on the Tuesday, and she would be glad of his help.

They closed the door of the cottage and Tommy handed the keys over. He thought of keeping it on and living in it himself, but decided against it. This gave him the opportunity to go back to sea, back into the Merchant Navy. He was happy with the keeper job for now.

The house was five minutes' walk from the beach. Bessie never went on the beach, but she liked to sit by the sea, in the little cafe, and face the sea. When she had the time she and Kate would walk down to the prom, and she would sit by the sea. She felt more at ease knowing she didn't have to rely on Joe's job to keep a roof over their heads.

On The Island

- 10 -

Joe went back on duty at the lighthouse. He had been in the job now for a year and nine months, and he could do the job as well as Tommy. They were into their third day when the storm broke and swept the Island.

"This storm is never ending." Kate said to her mum as she took the umbrella from the cupboard where they kept their coats and outdoor shoes.

She was catching the tram for school she said cheerio, and went out of the door.

Bessie was cleaning the house, before she was due to start the afternoon shift at the cafe. Kate was doing a few hours' work at the cafe, when she finished school.

It was the day that Mr Campbell should visit the lighthouse bringing them fresh meat and bottled water, Joe was looking forward to receiving his mum's baking and his football magazine. The lamps were being cleaned; Joe and Tommy were both in the lamp room.

"We are almost finished here, I will make some tea and we can have a break." said Tommy. He went down to put the kettle on. He called Joe down when the tea was ready. They were listening to the wireless and the weather news.

"If this weather keeps up I doubt if Mr Campbell will be coming today." said Tommy.

The weather forecast said the weather is to continue for a few days. They accepted that there would be no visit with the provisions. They had plenty of tins and juice, some bottled water, and they had tap water. They would have to make do with what they have for a few days.

Bessie caught the bus to take her into Burnt Island, to start her shift at the cafe. Kate would be joining her after school; she was working a few hours with Bessie, because Peggy had the evening off.

The rain was lashing down on her umbrella, it didn't stop Bessie had to straighten the umbrella twice already the wind eventually turned it inside out, she struggled with it to try to put it back the right way. The tram was coming, so she just put it into the trash box by the tram stop.

She boarded the tram and sat near the door. The tram past the cafe and the stop was almost on the door. Her mind strayed to Joe he would be working the lamps at the lighthouse, no matter how bad the storm was. She realized she was near her stop and she rose up from her seat to let the conductor know she was getting off the tram.

She arrived at the cafe and Peggy greeted her, she was waiting to leave. Bessie muttered.

"Let me get my coat off." but her words fell on deaf ears. Peggy was already going through the door that led to the main street.

She put her apron on and approached the first customer.

Joe and Tommy were having their free time and were listening to a play on the wireless. They set the lamps to auto, but because of the storm they were checking the room more than usual.

They decided to do some checking of the doors down in the basement. Joe suggested that they put some wet suits on because they had to go outside a few times to adjust the lamps. It was when he noticed a trickle of water coming in under the door. Tommy suggested putting some sand bags around it. They would keep their eye on it. They would check it again in an hour.

Bessie was in the cafe, but because she had no customers Peggy went home. Kate was due to start her shift in half an hour. A few customers came into the shop they were day trippers. Kate sympathized with them about the weather. They were not bothered about the weather they spent the day in the pub out of the rain.

Kate arrived for her shift and started serving them.

Tommy placed some more sand bags around the door of the lighthouse; it was letting in a little water. He would check it again in an hours' time. The lamps were revolving on auto. Joe was reading and Tommy was listening to a play on the wireless.

They had a hot drink sitting on a tray beside them. The play finished and Tommy remembered he was checking the sand bags. They seemed okay, and he came back upstairs and continued listening to the wireless.

"I wish this weather would get better." He said. He didn't want to alarm Joe, by voicing his fears. Joe was enjoying the story he was reading.

Bessie was indoors, it was too wet to go out. She had been out in morning for some shopping. The storm seemed to be getting worse. The wind was howling, and fierce. It was sweeping the Island, destroying everything within its path.

It was an hour later, when Tommy discovered that the first floor was under water.

"I will call the Coast Guard." said Tommy. He used the normal procedure but there was no answer. When he couldn't get through he called on the emergencies.

"May day, May day." but the line was dead.

"The lines must be affected by the storm." Said Joe.

Tommy being in charge decided he would try again in an hour, he saw the look on Joe's face and changed it to half an hour.

The tried to pump, the water out with a generator and when that didn't work they tried by hand to keep the water down and from rising.

Tommy tried again to reach the Coast Guard, he still couldn't get through. They waded through the water to the equipment room.

"Grab a life jacket and put it on." he said

They both waded through the water and went back upstairs. Tommy kept trying to reach the Coast Guard.

Bessie was unaware that Joe was in danger although he wasn't far from her mind. None was aware that there was anything wrong at the lighthouse.

The Keepers Are Trapped on the Lighthouse

- 12 -

Tommy was trying to contact the Coast Guard, but the lines were down. He joined Joe in the lamp room. They had enough food because of the tins they had in stock.

"I will try again in a couple of hours." Joe nodded not showing Tommy his fear. He was trying to put a brave face on the matter. He glanced at the sea it was pretty rough and he didn't like the thought of having to be rescued from it.

Tommy was feeling much the same. He was wishing he didn't have the responsibility of making the decisions. He hoped he would make the right one's if he had to.

Mr Campbell had been trying to reach the keepers but the lines being down he couldn't. He was worried about how they would be coping with the storm. They were both very young and had not much experience as keepers.

"At last" said Joe and handed over to Tommy.

"Mr Campbell, The lighthouse is flooded. The first floor is under water."

"Prepare to abandon the lighthouse, leave it by climbing down the escape ladder, when the life boat comes".

Tommy and Joe went up to the lamp room where the escape ladder.

They waited by the lamp room, another message came in.

"The life boats can't get out, it's too dangerous, and we will get to you as soon as we can. Sit by the radio."

The rocks around the lighthouse were the problem. The life boat wouldn't be able to navigate around it without crashing into them. They would have to wait for the sea to be calmer. The boys went back to the lounge. They played some board games to take their minds off the situation.

They didn't get any more news and they decided that there would be nothing more until daylight, so they went to sleep one on each chair by the fire and the radio.

In the morning Joe informed Tommy that the water had risen a little, Tommy was attending to the lamps and he looked at the rocks below. The sea was no calmer. It looked rougher.

He went back to the radio; again there was no sound the lines were down again. They heard a loud crash.

Bessie hears that Joe is trapped on the lighthouse.

Bessie was almost finished her shift at the cafe, down by the pier in Burnt sand, Kate came in all flustered and crying.

"What's happened?"

"It's Joe he is trapped on the lighthouse, and it's flooded?"

She took the paper from Kate and read the story for herself.

She locked the door, and waited for the last customer to leave the shop

They both went to Mr Campbell office, to see what the latest news of how the life boats were coping with the rescue

They were at the lighthouse again, although the sea was rough, and the waves were crashing against the rocks. They tried to rescue the keepers but the waves were too high for them to climb down the escape ladder. They would be washed against the rocks and carried out to see.

Bessie and Kate continued to wait for news, they spent the night in cafe, and it was nearer than going all the way home to come back in the morning.

At the lighthouse Joe went to investigate what the crash was they heard from upstairs. It was the bedroom window. There was glass everywhere. Tommy joined him. They could see all the damage that was caused by the storm.

And telephone wires uprooted and strewn across the island. The water continued to rise in the first floor and another day lost. They were still trapped.

Bessie and Kate handed over the keys to Peggy, the cafe owner. She had heard about the keepers on the news. She gave them the time off to go and wait for news. Bessie was anxious, and fear took hold of her. She had always feared that Joe wouldn't return from the sea. He was still out there, trapped.

Tommy was back on the radio the Coast Guard.

"Please hurry, the water is rising, and we don't know how long we can hang on."

The coast guard and Mr.Campbell tried to reassure the young keepers. The true fact was that they couldn't get near the lighthouse. The waves were too high and when they tried to anchor a rope to it. The wind just blew the rope back. They just didn't have a clue how to get the keepers off.

Bessie waited and she spent another night at the cafe. They both took their rosary beads from their handbags and prayed for the two young keepers. Bessie was trying to keep a brave face for Kate's sake. Kate was fearfully upset.

Back at the lighthouse Joe tried to go about his business as usual it was the day for him to do the Cooking he looked at the selection of tins he had to see if he could spice them up a little, and Tommy was in the lamp room looking for the rescue boats.

"Joe the lamp room is breaking away from the lighthouse." Tommy cried in a panic

They both grabbed a life jacket and were climbing down the escape ladder. They had no choice, but to go into the water. They heard a loud rash and they jumped from the ladder; and swam away from the lighthouse. The water was freezing. Joe was finding it difficult to keep afloat. They were in the water about ten minutes, when the lighthouse came crashing down into the water, and the sea was in darkness.

Bessie was beside herself with worry; it was Kate who was reassuring her Mother this time.

"Don't cry mum Joe will be all right." But Bessie could only see the worse of the situation.

"Please don't take my son." she cried in vain.

Joe was in darkness He had lost sight of Tommy when the light went out on the lighthouse, when it crashed into the sea. He cried for Tommy.

"Tommy gives me a sound are you OK?"

"I'm OK But I'm tired Joe."

They kept calling to each other and for help in case the life boats were out looking for them.

Bessie was still by the pier waiting for news; she heard one of the rescuers say they still could've the keepers. Darkness was coming down, and the thought of Joe been out there all night was unbearable.

The lifeboats were back out for the last trip before abandoning the search. They were about to turn back. They heard a faint cry.

"Over here."

"They had found them."

The life boat picked the keepers up into the boat from the sea. They were exhausted from the trying to keep afloat and the sea constantly crashing against their bodies.

The Ambulance was waiting for the lifeboat to come into the pier.

They arrived and were driven straight to hospital, Kate went in the Ambulance with Joe, but was only allowed to see him for ten minutes. Joe fell asleep while Bessie was at his bed.

Joe and Tommy were allowed home after a good night's sleep

Joe came to terms He would sign on, but before going back he would spend some time with his mum and sister Kate, sland. The lighthouse was gone; his mother didn't need to worry about him keeping a roof over their heads. They had a house which didn't belong to Joe's job. He was free to go back to working in the Merchant Navy. He would sign on, but before going back he would spend some time with his mum and sister Kate, on Burn Island.

Short Story

My Early Years
Working in the Mill

- 1 -

I lived with my grandmother, and I was proud to be working and bringing home a wage. What I didn't know was that she gave it back to me in pocket money and bus fares. I lived in Motherwell and my job was in Crossford Lanark. I had travel on two buses, One from Motherwell to Hamilton and another Crossford. The journey took an hour. My story is in the year 1956 and I lived in Motherwell Lanarkshire Scotland.

My grandmother was very sick, and she called me into her bedroom.

"Molly I want you to leave the farm."

"Why? I like the farm." She continued her request.

"It's not the just about liking it. You have to travel too far and you will not be able to afford to keep yourself. All your wages go on bus fares. Promise you will think about it?"

I left the room grumbling.

Bill my uncle, I never called him uncle said,

"You will have to leave, my maw is worried about you, and she isn't well."

I looked at him in disbelief, my grandmother always coughed, and had bouts of sickness, but she always managed to get well again.

My aunt had a friend who lived a few doors away from us offered to speak for me in the mill, and get me a job. I was to start in the drawing room. I went into my job the next day and told my boss I had to leave. I didn't have to give notice, and he produced my cards and my tax P45 on Friday the same week.

I was accompanying Rima and Mary to the mill on my first day until I found friends of my own. They both were family friends. I was a lot younger than them.

"I didn't get on the bus and had to walk to town to get the bus, because Big Annie pushed me back in the queue." Said Mary.

"Who is big Annie and why did she push you?" "I asked excitedly." But the bus was coming and we had to run to the bus stop, and the conversation was lost.

***

I entered the DRAWING ROOM. It was separated from the rest of the factory. I was led by the top manager into the room, and handed over to Herbert the over looked. The noise of the machines were deafening.

"This is Lizzie, she will show you the ropes." And he left me. I thought he was abrupt, and Lizzie answered as though she read my mind.

"It's alright he has not had a youngster like you before in his charge."

I looked around and she wasn't kidding me. Everybody in the room looked old. They were all old enough to be my mother. She interrupted my thoughts and set me to weighing bobbins of wool to go on to the machines. I picked this first task quite quick.

"Do you swear?" Lizzie suddenly asked.

I Looked at her and thought to myself,

"Doesn't everybody at the age of sixteen? "But I wasn't going to tell her I swore so I answered.

"No."

A few minutes later I released a leaver on the weighing scales by mistake and sent the bobbin crashing to the floor on to my foot, and let a few choice swear words Loose from my mouth. Hobbling around in a circle.Lizzie looked at my foot and when she was satisfied that there was no damage done said.

"I thought you didn't swear?"

Herbert came to the machine and put a bobbin on the bench and said something to me and abruptly walked away.

"What did he say?" I anxiously asked Lizzie, Herbert was English spoken, and a far different language from my Scottish tongue.

"It's Ok he just wants you to take the bobbin to the office for him."

I went to the office with the bobbin, and came back and settled to the work again. My next task was to put two bobbins on top of each other and wheel them to the next machine. it was tricky at first, because the bobbins kept coming apart, but I eventually mastered it and placed the two bobbins at a machine. I was talking to Lizzie and the lady came up to me and took my hand and took the two bobbins I had just placed on the next machine. It was at the wrong machine and she showed me where it should have been placed. She was a well-dressed lady almost too dressed for a factory. She covered her skirt with a smock. There was a lot of oil and wool of the machines, but she looked spotless and more well-dressed than the other women. I discovered she was Isa Mary was talking about in the morning.

I mumbled "Thanks." And returned to Lizzie. I was furious how dare she treat me as a child. Lizzie saw my anger and said.

"Isa is lovely she wouldn't mean to offend you." "I wasn't listening to her."

"what would she know she is old?"

It was near dinner time and Lizzie's daughter came to see her. She introduced me to Betty. and she suggested that I meet up with her during the lunch break. I agreed to meet Betty in the canteen. I was among people of my own age at least for a half hour.

I was working on the machine in the afternoon and I was shown how to piece together two ends of wool and join them together. I had not joined the wool right and this lady came over to the machine and abruptly stopped it. Annie was correcting my mistake. It was none other than the person Mary was talking about in the morning. Big Annie. Oh how I wished at that moment I was on the farm working in my tomato houses